The View from Deacon Hill

JACK S. SCOTT

The View
from Deacon Hill

NEW HAVEN AND NEW YORK
TICKNOR & FIELDS
1981

Copyright © 1981 by Jack S. Scott

First published in the USA in 1981 by
Ticknor & Fields

Published in Great Britain by
William Collins Sons & Co. Ltd.

Library of Congress Cataloging in Publication Data

Scott, Jack S
The view from Deacon Hill.
"A Joan Kahn book."
I. Title.
PR6069.C589V5 1981   813'.54   80–28532
ISBN 0–89919–033–2

Printed in the United States of America

P   10   9   8   7   6   5   4   3   2   1

The View from Deacon Hill

CHAPTER 1

It was fortunate, from the young man's point of view, that even in his lover's after-swoon his basic survival sense remained alert. It is so in all the cunning bent, of course; they never truly relax. He did not hear the car's approach, it crept down the hill with engine turned off; but when the time came, he moved fast.

The ground upon which the motor-caravan stood was not exactly a lay-by. That word suggests main highways, juggernaut lorries, cars drawing in bearing the strange people who seem to drive out expressly to sit in lay-bys, consuming sandwiches and absorbing out of plastic cups something horrible tipped from plastic flasks. This was no highway. There was nothing here at all but green grass and a few trees, hedges, fields, heather and ling on the uplands. Not even a farm within half a mile. Whoever made the bald earth margin beside the lane did it by driving over and over until the grass wore off, probably making space to turn unwieldy agricultural vehicles. Here the van stood on this lovely evening, and for very good reason.

The reason was blonde, twenty-two years old. The young man had been trying to make her for some time. Personable young men, unattached and with money enough to live off the high hog and to run not only a smart motor-caravan but a Jaguar too for the daily chores, do not normally meet with serious resistance. This one did, from this girl. Fact is, the coolness she had shown towards him until now reflected truly the way she felt. She simply hadn't fancied him, and she was a girl with money of her own, no need to open up for a good time. But the hook goes deeper when lust is denied, especially when the man is seldom denied. The masculine sexual ego is a very touchy thing, and lust denied feeds upon pique.

A whole month after he met her, before she said yes, all right, he could take her to the races. But she'd be going home afterwards. OK? If not—no go.

So today was the race meeting. He took her in the motor-caravan, it being very convenient for what he had in mind; telling her, when she expressed surprise, that the Jag had broken down. They had a pleasant day, champagne lunch in a good restaurant and the races after. En route for home he turned off the main road, away from the stream of homegoing punters into this narrow, hedge-bordered lane. 'Where are we going?' she asked.

'Short cut,' he said. 'Better than the main road. There's a good pub, we can have a look at the sunset.'

'I'm getting hungry,' she said.

'Plenty of grub aboard. All we need's a parking place.' Another great convenience, with a caravan: stock it up, you are self-sufficient for a long time.

'Who's going to do the cooking?' A desirable blonde, out with a man who has crinkle-lined pockets, does not expect to end the day parked in a country lane, fending him off while she slaves over a hot butane gas-cooker. She expects to be cherished.

This was by no means his first blonde. He followed her thinking. 'No problem. There's a good restaurant, before you get to the pub.'

For all he truly knew, the lane might end by plopping into a river. He had travelled it only as far as this lay-by, where he had spent a frolicsome night once before with another blonde. Many such quiet places were marked down in his mind. Apart from its value to certain nefarious enterprises, a very good reason for having the van was: bed stood always handy; and he could not, for the sake of low profile and because of his parents, have a stream of nubile young women entering by night the beautiful apartment in the luxury block, and leaving it in the morning under the boot-button eye of respectable neighbours. Jealousy ensures that respectable women hiss over things like that like geese untupped by a fancied gander.

Who knows why a woman, hitherto touch-me-not, suddenly yields? He had a nicely practised technique, yes, and probably the wine with lunch and a few drinks since out of carried stock had some effect. Probably, too, he was far better company than she had expected, because he knew how to charm a woman when he wanted her, as well as he knew how to terrorize one. But these, one would think, are hardly reason enough in themselves. Women are, and it is a truism, utterly unpredictable. Most likely she simply happened to come on heat. Perhaps she, in turn, was piqued and twitching because against all expectation he had not made a pass all day.

Within half an hour of parking in that lay-by she was naked on the double bed which makes down from the dinette at the touch of a button; he naked on top of her, pretty coloured curtains drawn over the windows and across behind the cab seats, denying interior goings-on to anybody peering through the windscreen. He found her good. They brought each other with gasps and low moans to crying-out conclusion, and went together into their separate swoon. And then, quite suddenly, his unsubmersible senses prickled up. He raised his head; looked over his own naked shoulder to the door at the back of the van.

The inside handle, connected to the outside handle, was moving downward, slowly. Stealthily. With a jolt of alarm he knew that he had neglected, in horny haste, to do the thing he always did when he would be unguarded within the van: lock it. He did not pause to ponder who was this, come creeping. So many possibles. He reached out for the wrench, the very heavy metal wrench kept beside the bed, ever handy. A heavy wrench in a caravan cannot be classed by any nosey copper as an offensive weapon. It is a maintenance tool.

The door was opening. A head came in; a bulky figure glimpsed, feet obviously on the outside step; a hand holding what had to be a gun, warily. Shoulders came through, hunched, the head remaining bent because the young man had not raised the elevating roof to give full height. Golden light outside, spilling from a glorious sunset. The hills here are famous vantage points for view-ing the sunset. Inside, the light diffused by drawn cur-tains. The head moved, seeking to orientate. All this in two seconds.

The young man twisted on the bed, one lithe, imposs-ible turn; smashed with panic force. The massive wrench struck the head just as it lowered to use its eyes for guiding a foot from the step to the van's carpeted floor. 'What— what—?' the girl said, awakened with a jolt; and the head gave out a tock like a clouted pumpkin, the mouth made a grunt, the body fell back from the door, heavily on to the ground like a dropped barley-sack.

'What—what—?' she said again, jerking up; and folded her arms across pretty breasts to cover them, as girls will automatically, startled naked out of sleep. But the young man flattened her again, scrambling up her body to fling himself through the curtains drawn between living quarters and cab; tumbling over the back of the van-wide bench seat; scrambling into position behind the steering-wheel; twisting the ignition key, left in the lock.

A car stood in the lane. He saw it through the wind-screen. As his engine came to life, so did the other; as the van moved forward as fast as he could force it, so did the car. Faster, having better acceleration. Before he could check—draw back—do anything—he was committed. He could only charge up that lane in the wake of the car. No possibility of turning, there simply was not enough room.

Not once he came out from the bald earth patch; and this he'd done by reflex action, before his brain was thinking.

So there they were, charging up the lane. Nobody else about—nowhere to go along this lane, it merely winds between moorland and sheep-fields, connecting the A classified road with the B road running roughly parallel a mile away. Above it the wide sky, golds and greens and yellows and reds flaming as the sun went down.

If this was a hit job, it was thoroughly botched. Bad enough, the hit-man hit; but what induced the men still in the car to take off like that? A few yards forward, a halt; and they could have bottled the van into the lay-by. Two of them, presumably professionals, could surely have handled one young man in his birthday suit?

Possibly it was sheer surprise that threw them, when their buddy with the gun fell suddenly into the road backwards and the young man scrambled naked into the driving seat, there to make fumbles obviously designed to start the engine and put the van in motion. Perhaps they felt they would be better off out of the vicinity, changing their minds three hundred yards along the twisty lane when professionalism overtook panic and they realized the bird had by no means flown. Even now, when they stopped the car in the middle of the road they did not choose the best possible situation.

Agreed, it was round an almost dog-leg bend, which made for an element of surprise; but there were narrower places farther along, and the bordering hedge so reinforced by stout trees that not even the most daring or terrified driver could get by. Presumably, they knew no more about the lane than the young man did.

It cannot be said of the young man, either, that he reacted with ice-cool intelligence; but then, of course, few people do, shocked out of after-doze by a character with a gun in his hand and impelled to drive naked up a small lane at sunset. Panicked, he didn't even see the absurdity of charging off like that, one after the other. He didn't even wonder where they were both going. Not that he had a lot of time to wonder. He came round that dog-leg bend and there was the car, slap in the middle of the road; two open doors sticking out like wings, two characters clambering forth. He trod hard on the brake.

The girl had arisen. She had stuck her head through the drawn curtains, holding them together under her chin like a coy maiden on a very old bathing-machine postcard. She swayed to the swaying of the truck, crying 'What — what — what's going on?' And she fell over sideways as the van leaned, shrieking round the bend; banged her sweet nose, poor thing, on a bulkhead as tyres squealed to the grip of good brakes.

The young man did not even know she was there. He saw the car — he saw the characters coming forth — he slammed the rig into reverse. But reverse a motor-caravan hastily back round a dog-leg bend? Never. In a praying panic? Never. Not a hope, especially when drawn curtains cut off all backward view except what shows in the wing mirror. Came a crunch, as the back of the van hit the grass mound bordering the lane. Sobbing, he slammed the gear lever forward again.

One of the characters — the one who had been travelling in the passenger's seat — was coming now, running. The young man stamped the accelerator, pointing the van straight at him. The character dived very nimbly sideways, into the hedge. His oppo was less lucky.

The girl had clutched the seatback now. Blonde hair bird-nested, her face came again through the curtains, blood redder than her lipstick trickling from delicate nostrils. 'Stop it — stop it —' she was shrieking. And still the young man didn't know she was there. He aimed the van at the too-small gap between offside of the car and the grass-mound border topped by the hedge. The character who had stayed by the open door saw him coming and tried to do something—scramble back in, leap over the bonnet, anything that would get him to the near side. Offside room would be all taken up. But the inside appurtenances of automobile doors are tricky things, and especially if you wear a chunky-knit jumper they will catch you if they can. The door-handle grabbed his sleeve.

He never had a chance to free it. The van bounced, one side up the grass mound, tearing through the hedge with a rending, cracking, cellulose-scagging noise. The other side hit him, squashing him against that door; wrecking its own bumper, smashing its own headlight, denting itself all down the side as it ripped on by. He hung for a second; dropped to the road.

The girl, clinging somehow, was screaming now. 'You've killed him—you've killed him—stop—stop—you hit him—'

'Shut up shut up shut up,' the young man babbled; and they went like the clappers away from there, stark naked and he with his foot hard down.

CHAPTER 2

On that day—it was a Saturday—Detective-Sergeant Alfred Stanley Rosher reported for duty to the town police station in very fair fettle at three o'clock in the afternoon. The hours worked by CID men are infinitely variable. They cop the occasional Saturday or Sunday off, but in general weekends mean nothing to them, and neither do normal knocking-off times. Engaged on a job, they simply work whatever hours it demands, taking time off when the kefuffle dies down. Thus, Sergeant Rosher had been working through all of yesterday and most of the night. Hence his late arrival. For the notable spring in his step there were two reasons.

First, he had cracked it. The case upon which he had been working—he would clear it today. Nice case, too, and not so big that kudos would pass to a superior rank. A string of small break-and-enters, warehouses and stores. A lightish van used, the same one each time, Forensic said when they did what they do with tyre marks. A small backhander yesterday to a whispering grass confirmed what he already knew in his mind—the name of the little operator—and with it something he had not known: that he would be working most of the night.

Part of this time, then, the sergeant spent in a plain car parked unobtrusively close by an afore-whispered warehouse. Another part he spent copping Benny Judd in the act, as he moved to drive his laden van away. Frightened the little man out of his wits, jumping out on him like that. More hours passed while Benny was booked in, and asked by the sergeant, not once but many times, who sent him out and took the gear from him; because among Benny's many and varied deficiencies was a brain, one of which he had not got. He never had and never could plan even a single job, never mind a series; but he could pick any lock, he could get in anywhere. Benny declining to cough, the sergeant put the fear of God into him by outlining what he, Rosher, intended to say to the beak should he, Benny, maintain himself in his stupidity. He then wished the little man a comfortable night and took himself home to bed.

The phone rang about one o'clock, this afternoon. He took his time. Came in to the station at three. It was not the sort of triumph for which a man is elevated to the peerage; but it would sit on him quite nicely, and at just the right time.

So there is the first reason for good fettle. Second reason—and this was the one that had him humming tunelessly in the bathroom and during the donning of his durable blue serge suit—the grapevine that operates in every police station was murmuring. It said that he, ex-Detective-Inspector Old Blubbergut Rosher, bust down, alas, by the old Chief Constable, might—only might, mind you—shortly be shoved up again by the new one, to fill the hole when Detective-Inspector John (Bonker) Barclay retired.

Reason enough for tuneless humming. Almost unheard of, for a man to be bust down and win his way back. And this within two years of retirement. The stuff of legend; and, he told himself with the first unblemished self-approval he had felt since calamity smote him hip and thigh, all due to his own efforts. Agreed, there was an element of luck in his nobbling of the maniac who called himself The Avenger, and his triumph was somewhat qualified by his having buggered a highly expensive drugs operation at the same time; but luck comes only to the man who is ready and due; and if the bloody drugs squad camped out with a near-naked bird and looked like a degenerate Apache—naturally, it got busted.

It was characteristic of Rosher, who in his palmy days did not earn his nickname for nothing, that he should tend to over-approve his own part in success. The truth is: the new Chief Constable took over from the old Chief Constable at a time when Rosher, currently in hospital, was due to face a second disciplinary enquiry designed to break him forever. Studying papers, the new Chief found that designed was the operative word. Only a very biased judge could make the charges stick; and the old Chief Constable would have been judge.

He explored further; and decided, being an unusually humane man for one of exalted rank, that Rosher had fallen victim as much to condemnation in high places as to his own undoubted shortcomings. Rosher, chained tight to a CID room desk by the fierce, lion-headed man who meant to squeeze him to death, found the chain suddenly struck off and himself in the field again, the whip above cracking fair. He retook to his natural element like a duck long starved for water. Many routine cases he had worked on since, cracking most of them fair and square. As with this latest one.

In fact, more than Rosher's sensationally publicized copping of The Avenger—television loved it, and all the national papers; and without doubt it removed from the Chief's own gullet a nasty little hook—the very thing that swayed the Chief, who was indeed considering the sergeant's re-elevation, was the one factor that might have been expected to weigh against it: Rosher's impending retirement. A fair man, this Chief, and he thought about the pension. With reduction in rank comes reduction in pension. Whether Rosher deserved to be busted for one offence after so many years—his career record showed it—of sterling service was almost beside the point. Many policemen err as foolishly, and are not found out. Quite obviously, he was guiltless of the charges being prepared against him while he lay in hospital, put there by what had to be seen as an act of conspicuous bravery. The new Chief felt sympathy for Rosher, and he had both the will and the power, given opportunity, to make restitution. Along came The Avenger. And now the grapevine was humming.

So the sergeant came into the station at three o'clock on a warm, sunny Saturday, and if the tuneless humming did not actually percolate between his big, brown teeth, it still went on in his head. He suspended it to address Sergeant Barney Dancey, a veteran with the calm eyes that speak of a soul at rest (it cannot be seen in many policemen), on duty behind the enquiry desk.

'How do, Barney. How's your belly off for spots?'

Sergeant Barney—nobody ever called him by his surname, it was always Sergeant Barney, even from the schoolkids who adored his road safety lectures—looked up with no surprise in those blue, blue eyes. Once, even he would have mentally staggered at the incongruity of a jesting Rosher; as Romans did, perhaps, when Pilate tried for laughs. But of late, since The Avenger, the sergeant had arrived often with a merry quip. Hoary, but merry. So he crinkled into a grin, saying: 'Not so bad, Alf. Yours?'

Sergeant Rosher, passing on, patted where the little pot had been growing under the calorie assault of his fat wife's cooking. Gone now, fat wife and little pot both. One home to Mother, weeping; the other flattened by a diet of lonely baked beans, boiled eggs and singed chops, consumed in a dusty kitchen with crinkle chips. 'No spots here, my son. Nothing but solid muscle.'

Box-toed shoes carried him on into the passage, over clacking lino to where young Detective-Inspector Alec Cruse was just coming from the office that once was his own. Preceding him, waiting now while he closed the door, was another young man, equally tall but skinnier. Gangling. That's the word.

'Ah—Sergeant Rosher,' said young Cruse. 'Just the man I was hoping to see.'

He spoke with less of the embarrassed constraint that had come down between them since Rosher's busting; when he, junior investigating officer on the case where Old Blubbergut touched up a publican's wife, had been forced to supply the eye-witness account that brought the old bugger low, afterwards finding himself promoted and given Rosher's old room to keep up to strength the establishment holed by Rosher's downgrading. Rosher's Avenger triumph, coming after so long a time of humiliation, had helped; and now, the whisper reckoned, the old bugger might be up level again before long. The situation had eased considerably, to young Cruse's great relief.

'Uh-huh?' said Rosher. Quite impossible, for these two

now ever to be on Alf-and-Alec terms. Not that they ever were. Old Blubbergut, in the days when Cruse was a young and tender underling, addressed him as lad, or son, or even sonny, normally with a sarcastic edge; and he saw to it that he himself was approached with proper respect. Now, each avoided even the other's rank, if they could.

'You know Mr O'Hopper, I expect?' said Cruse.

'Not personally, no. I've read about him in the local paper, I knew he was over, but I've hardly been inside the place for a week.'

'Oh. I thought you'd have met. Mr O'Hopper, this is Sergeant Rosher. Sergeant-Patrolman O'Hopper.'

The gangling young man shot out a gangling young hand. It met Sergeant Rosher's large and hairy offering and shook it up and down. 'Pleased to meet you, sir,' said a voice shaped somewhere across the Atlantic; and the young man's mind said: Jeez—the guy's a gorilla.

'Uh-huh,' said Rosher. The young man's wide, smiling mouth showed a plenitude of gleaming white, even teeth. All-American teeth, honed on T-bone steaks, Thanksgiving turkey and, presumably, blueberry pie. Rosher permitted a glimpse of his own brownstone incisors. Went that colour after German measles and never changed back. 'How do.'

'You brought little Benny Judd in last night, they tell me,' said Alec Cruse. He wore the smile of the host, angling matters the way he wants them to go.

'This morning.' Anything that happened before 9.30 a.m. today may be last night to you, lad. To me, I brought him in this morning.

Cruse corrected. 'This morning. Good. Mr O'Hopper is here to study our—er—procedure. Techniques. I was thinking you might like to—take him over, show him how we handle these matters. He's—er—attached to us for a few days, then he'll be going on to other departments.

Right, Mr O'Hopper?' He flashed his host's smile.

'Yeah. Guess so.' The eager teeth beamed forth more whitely yet.

'Ah,' said Sergeant Rosher.

'We're a bit quiet at the moment,' Cruse said. 'You seem to be the only one with a—er—an active assignment.' That's what Kojak had—assignments. 'So—yes. Well—that's it, then. If you'll go with Mr Rosher, then, Mr O'Hopper, I'm sure you'll have a—pleasant day.'

'Sure. Fine.' Never saw a man who looked so like you ought to feed him bananas. Look at the arms. Damn near down to the knees.

'Good. See you later, then. Thank you, Sergeant.' A last beam all round and Cruse turned away, patently relieved to have the visitor taken off his back.

'Hrrrmph,' said Sergeant Rosher; and he did the thing those who knew him braced against, when they saw it coming. He drew forth a great, off-white handkerchief— how napery standards fall when a fat wife leaves home— raised it to his wide nostrils and blew. Up and down the bare corridor the echoes galloped. Unprepared, the young man's teeth vanished for a second, while his eyes blinked rapidly. Jesus Christ, he thought.

Sergeant Rosher wiped; tucked the sheet away; coughed; removed the black Anthony Eden hat that rode low upon his simian brow; scratched with extended forefinger the top of a short-back-and-sided skull; replaced the hat in its original position. 'Yes,' he said. 'Well—if you're ready.'

'Yeup. Sure,' said the young man.

The sergeant led the way along the clacking compo-tiled passage between bare mustard-coloured walls to where the clack changed tone, naked stone stairs leading to a subterranean stone corridor. Three cells down here, and a custodian policeman sitting behind a deal table on a hard wooden chair. A man was singing in one of the cells, heartily enjoying the time between lunch-time drinking session and hangover.

' 'Afternoon, Charlie,' said Rosher.

'All right for some,' the policeman answered, cheer-fully morose. He got up; went with his bunch of big keys to the end cell and unlocked it. 'Ta,' said Rosher, walking in. The young patrolman followed. The custodian went back to his little wooden chair. The drunk started another chorus.

Little Benny Judd was lying full length on the cell bunk, his head pillowed on folded issue blankets. He sat up as they entered, blinking pop eyes set in a doughy, oddly unfinished face. His nose was a little blob, as though when he was being formed the Great Potter had been called away, and set him for firing in a hurry. Likewise, the muscular mechanism that keeps a mouth shut had obviously been overlooked. He sat slack-lipped and pop-eyed, blinking.

'Afternoon, Benny,' said Rosher. 'Lovely day, out there.'

'Listen, Mr Rosher,' the little man said. 'I bin finking.'

'I hoped you would, lad. I rather hoped you would.' Rosher spoke with huge joviality, brown teeth bare. Quite the Old Blubbergut of yesteryear, come again to where he could use the tone he always had used, speaking to little men sitting on cell bunks or facing him in an interview room.

'Who's that?' Benny pointed to the young, gangling man, standing by in a lightweight suit such as few British policemen wear.

'Mr O'Hopper,' the sergeant told him. 'He's come all the way from America, just to have a look at you.'

'America?' said Benny. 'I don't know nuffin about America. You can't pin nuffin on me about America. I never bin there. I can prove it.'

'You'd be surprised, lad, what I can pin on you. Remember what happened to Al Capone?'

'Mr Rosher, I swear it—I never bin to America.'

'Cool it, lad, cool it. Just my little joke. Stick to the matter in hand. Let me hear your innermost thoughts.'

'Oh. Yeah. Well—you wouldn't really say all them things you said you'd say to the beak, would you? You wooden be telling the troof.'

'Benny, Benny,' the sergeant said in jovial reproof, 'you mustn't suggest before a witness that I am a liar under oath. I shall merely point to your record and mention that you refused to cooperate with the police. Tell him what's undoubtedly true—that you're an habitual. An anti-social force, lad, entitled by your record to a dose of PD. That's twelve years, give or take a bit. Isn't it? On the other hand . . .'

A few minutes later the custodian relocked the cell door behind which Benny was beginning to eat his finger-nails to the quick, wondering whether PD wasn't rather better than what can happen to him who grasses. When they had mounted the stone stairs and were clacking together along the corridor, the patrolman said to the sergeant: 'Er—what's PD?'

'Preventative Detention. Old lag gets enough porridge, next time up he's habitual. PD, minimum twelve.'

'Ah. Uh-huh.' The patrolman walked on, mulling over the unfamiliar jargon delivered in an accent still strange to his ears. A week he had been here, of the month suddenly wished on him—awarded, they called it—as this end of an exchange visit between here and the town where he lived, which twinned with this one because they shared the same name and some mayor or someone long ago thought it would be a good idea. Since when, British boy scouts and girl guides had camped and frolicked (separately. Oh yes) occasionally in Pennsylvania fields, and American counterparts had camped and caught streaming colds in English ones. At this very moment a Sergeant James Batey, British half of the exchange, was rolling around in far-flung Pennsylvania with a morning-shift patrol and wondering if these gum-chewing buggers with the gun on the hip really did shoot first and ask questions after; and if so, what sort of answers did they get?

'Fancy a trip in the country?' the gorilla-man asked.

'Sure. Great.'

'We'll go and pick up our Mastermind.'

Some kind of a gadget? Computer, maybe? Or was it one of these British-style jokes? No—get with it—the old guy meant the guy behind the little guy. 'Yeah. Great. Er—do you have another name, besides Russia?'

'Rosher,' said Rosher. 'The name's Rosher. Hrrmph. Alfred.'

'Sorry,' the young man said. 'It's the—er—you know—the accent. Ain't wholly got the hang of it yet, kinda still bugs me. Er—by the way, it ain't O'Hopper. It's O. Hopper. The O's kind of an initial letter. First name's Gaylord. Gaylord O. Hopper.'

'Ah.' Bloody hooray, thought Alfred Stanley Rosher, they don't half come up with some names. As a matter of amusement, he asked: 'What does the O stand for?'

'Nothing. It's just an O, my dad thought it sounded better than plain Gaylord Hopper.' The beautiful teeth were flashing that grin again.

'You were O'Hopper in the *Evening Courier*.'

'Yeah. That's newspapers. Now everybody's doing it. Okay if I call you Al, sir?'

Rosher's mind took a sudden leap back to the only time in his life when he had dealings with Americans closer than putting the odd tourist on the way to the famous sunset. Italy, during the war, when as a rigorously pipe-clayed and polished military policeman he spent some days cut off with a detachment of them in the Appenines, Germans not far away and nobody able to fight because of the blizzard. They called him Al, he remembered. First names were an American tradition, they even called their officers Bill and Eddie. He'd looked down his nose at first; but in the end he had come to like being Al. And by Christ, when it came to fighting their way out of there, they'd known how to do it. Fancy—they could have been this young bugger's father. Well—one of 'em could.

'I can stand it if you can,' he said.

'Sure. Yeah. Fine,' said the patrolman. 'Makes it kind of cozier. I'll just collect my camera.' He peeled off, went through the door into the CID room.

Well, of course, Rosher thought, finding a bubble of pure amusement bobbing about in his general good humour—when did you ever see a Yank without a camera? He moved on to the reception area, and the door. To Sergeant Barney Dancey, writing something in the big black Incidents Book, he said: 'Going out, Barney. Hutton Fellows, to pick up Henry Croker.'

Barney glanced up. 'Henry? Been a naughty boy again, has he, after all this time? Haven't seen him since he moved out of town. How long ago was that, two years? What's he been up to?' He sounded mildly regretful. He always did regret the shortfalling of mankind, and God knows he'd seen enough of it, all those years in blue serge. And still that limpid faith in his baby-blue eyes. Amazing.

'Been putting our Benny up to things. I'm taking the Yank with me.'

'Nice boy,' said Sergeant Barney.

Young Hopper came from the CID room, festooned with camera, light meter and binoculars. He grinned at Sergeant Barney and said: 'Hi, Sarge.'

'Hi,' said Sergeant Barney. 'Have a pleasant trip, the country's beautiful.'

'Yeah. Sure,' the patrolman said, and passed from the building in company with Rosher, who actually stood aside and waved him on first through the door. Of course he was a guest, but even so it's not the sort of thing that happens every day.

The country is indeed lovely on the road out to and way beyond Hutton Fellows. Farmland at first, with two pretty villages. Then the moors, criss-crossed with little lanes and sheep tracks and purple in autumn when the heather blooms. Behind and all around stand the great blue hills, with the main highway winding through the valleys and minor roads clambering steeply over the tops. Young Hopper enjoyed the ride. Not much conversation—the monkey man didn't seem much for talking—but you could tell he enjoyed it, if you were Rosher in the driving seat of the unmarked official sedan, by the way he gazed out of the window, murmuring 'Well, I'll be damned,' and 'Will you look at that,' and 'Holy cow..'

Mr Henry Croker lived with his wife and two horse-mad daughters in a rather lovely old farmhouse just beyond the village. He did not farm, the surrounding land was rented to a man who did and the great barn was used by him, and by the hands employed by the Hon. David Lawney, whose land marched alongside. But he grew great roses. They nodded fatly, perfuming the early evening air as the two men trod a manicured gravel driveway up to the imposing eighteenth-century front door where Mr Croker awaited them, sitting in a deckchair with beer and wearing tweed.

He showed no agitation. He said: 'Good evening, Mr Rosher. Surprise, surprise. It's been a long time. All of two years, isn't it? What can we do for you?'

'How do, Henry,' the sergeant said. 'Nice evening. Your roses look well. Nice place you sorted out. Just came to have a look in your barn.'

'Bring a warrant with you?'

Rosher returned benign smile for benign smile. 'Now, now, Henry—let us not be obstructive.'

Mr Croker sighed resignedly. 'Oh well,' he said, 'Nobody wins them all. No doubt you'd enjoy a glass of beer afterwards?' He turned his bald head to where his wife, just popped out, stood on the doorstep twisting her hands together. 'Darling, will you fetch some beer for these gentlemen? You remember Mr Rosher, no doubt? And don't bother about dinner for me, I think I shall not be here.'

They left in half an hour, after inspection of the barn loft and beer taken leisurely. It seemed to Patrolman Hopper that this kind of thing must have become so familiar over the years that it had acquired a certain tradition of conduct. After Sergeant Rosher's brief uh-huh when it was uncovered, nobody alluded to the surprisingly heterogeneous collection of merchandise stored beneath the hay. He left with the picture imprinted on his retina of a gorgeous oak-beamed olde Englishe living-room—which Mr Croker kindly permitted him to photograph—and of the two daughters, who came in hard-hatted and riding-breeched, breasts bobbing unfettered beneath silk shirts. There's money enough for silk shirts for girls with a father who knows how to direct a few little men, and has learned to take the rough with the smooth.

It was all very civilized. The only one who seemed in any way disturbed was the wife, who tended to twitch; but even she, when time came for leaving, merely pecked her husband's cheek and requested that he look after himself. The two daughters also kissed him. One said, 'Be good, Daddy;' the other: 'We'll see you when we see you then, Dodykins.' And they all expressed a hope that Patrolman Hopper would enjoy his stay in England.

Rosher, when they reached the car, used the radio to contact the station, asking that men be sent with a truck to collect the goodies stashed in the barn. He then put the wheels in motion and drove away, himself and Hopper in the front seats, Mr Croker waving to his waving women from the back, just as though they were off for a trip to the seaside.

'Do you grow roses in America, Mr Hopper?' the bald

man asked as they travelled the lanes.

'Not me personally,' the young man replied. Seemed a funny way to make an arrest, no argument, no frisking for guns. 'People do.'

'You should,' said Mr Croker. 'There's great spiritual solace in roses. Purity in a world too often, alas, lacking in the quality. One does not expect to learn, Mr Rosher, who shopped one?'

'One wouldn't if one did, Henry,' said Rosher, still enormously jovial. 'Would one? We never divulge our sources of information, you know that.'

Mr Croker sighed. Addressed the patrolman again. 'If I have a fault, Mr Hopper, it consists in my employing the wrong people. But what can one do? The choice is limited. And one feels a certain responsibility to provide for our weaker brethren, with gainful employment.'

Was he serious? Hopper couldn't tell. With diligent study, a man in time can come to right assessment; but how do you tell, after only one week, if a man is speaking more than extreme unction? Strange race, the British. Peculiar sense of humour.

Rosher was grinning. He, too, addressed Hopper. 'He does that all right. There's not a tea-leaf in the manor doesn't cop for him, one way or another.'

'Mr Rosher,' said Croker mildly, 'there has been no allegation against me whatsoever for more than two years.'

'I didn't say you're not a crafty old sod, Henry, did I?' Rosher spoke to Hopper again. 'I thought we'd go back over the hills—the sun'll be setting, time we get there. You might like to see it, while we're here.'

'Great,' said Patrolman Hopper. Wait till he told the boys back home about these two characters. Wait till he told his wife tonight. She'd roll about.

'Wonderful sight,' said Mr Croker fruitily. 'Breath-taking, on an evening like this.'

Two or three miles before this lane would connect with the main road, they turned off it into a by-lane which in a little while rose so steeply that even the powerful police car took it in very low gear, grinding slowly. 'Charabanc parties go out of control on this hill every summer, Mr Hopper,' Mr Croker said. 'Old age pensioners, mostly, out on day trips. Bizarre way to go, one always feels, in the twilight of one's days. One often wonders about life after death.'

Half the time you had to concentrate real close to know what the hell they were talking about.

The view from that hill is truly superb at any time when mist and rain is not blotting it out. Mile upon mile of glorious country and a glitter of sea in the far distance. At sunset you wouldn't believe it. The rocks up here are nationally famous, of course, great conglomerations of them eroded and twisted into fantastic shapes by the millions of years of wind and weather since the earth hiccuped them up; known now by such inane and piddling titles as The Three Bears, The Bishop's Seat (it does look strangely like a well-nourished arse) and, inevitably, Lovers' Leap.

They left the car at the side of the lane and walked, Mr Croker coming along completely unfettered, chatting away like an old friend. There is a vantage point near the huge, grim monolith called The Horse's Head. Gaylord O. Hopper gazed out from there, and he murmured: 'Holy cow!'

Well he might. There was enough cloud, small cumulus and a dappling of fine-weather high cirrus, to provide gilt-edged relief in lovely greys and beiges to the wide sky vastly painted in reds and greens and golds, right up to cerulean blue.

'We have a saying, Mr Hopper,' said Mr Croker. 'Red sky at night, shepherd's delight. Plenty of delight there, eh?' He spoke with the strange pride natives show in natural phenomena, as if their own efforts had planned and shaped it.

Young Hopper was not unduly impressed by the rock formations. They do these things much better in the States, and he was a man who had seen the Painted Desert and teetered on the rim of the Grand Canyon; but the peculiarly British quality of colour flooded over a green, green world—this was really something.

He fumbled his binoculars out of their case; scanned the terrain for a moment; said to Rosher: 'You wanna hold these a minute, Al? I have to take a couple of shots.'

Rosher accepted the binoculars. The American readied his camera and began to snap; moved a fair distance to bring rocks into the foreground. Mr Croker chuckled indulgently. 'Delightful people, the Americans,' he said. 'They all have such beautiful teeth.'

The sergeant grunted, a rare good humour in the timbre of it. As a man given binoculars must, he raised them to his eyes. Cows and sheep in far fields, isolated buildings almost invisible to the naked eye, cars on the main road sprang sharp and clear up to him. Good glasses, cunningly wrought by clever Japanese in the seam-bursting city of Tokyo. A glint caught his eye from a lane somewhere between here and the far hills. As any soldier would testify, had he not just been hit by the sniper's bullet, a glint at sunset carries a long way. He retrained the glasses; and so, of course, he saw it all.

Not in fine detail, the lane was too far off. But he saw the glint, which came from what seemed to be the barrel of a gun, held by a crouching antlike figure approaching with what could only have been stealth a motor-caravan drawn up by the road on the far side. He saw the figure reach out and—obviously, it was proceeding with great caution—open the back door sufficiently for gun hand and head to vanish within. He saw a tiny leg bend to raise one foot to the level of the van floor; and suddenly the whole mannikin jerked violently backward, flopping to lie inert in the road.

'Bloody hell,' he said.

'What have you got?' asked Mr Croker. 'Nudists? They say there's a colony at Great Hampton.'

Rosher made no answer. He was concentrated. The van was beginning to move; and from dead ground on this side of the lane—he hadn't seen it before, because of the hedge—shot a car, taking off fast with the van after it. The entire ensemble was, beyond doubt, unorthodox.

This far, action had taken place south to north, across his line of vision. The dog-leg bend revealed a section of the lane running straight away from him, into the west and the sunset, vivid backlighting from which tended to mix solid body with shadow. He saw the speeding car round this bend and stop. Two toy figures emerged, in a hurry. One stayed by the left-open driver's door, the other began to run back along the lane as the van pelted round the dog-leg, and stopped, and backed up, fast. Too fast—driver in a panic. He saw—or thought he saw—the jerk when the van stopped, mound-rammed at the back. He saw it shoot forward.

The running man paused; waved an arm; dived, both feet off the ground, sideways into the hedge. The other tried—it was difficult, isolating visual details—to scramble up the side of the car. The van rushed on; canted dangerously, two wheels up the bank, ramming its way past; raced on, gathering speed; vanished round a further bend. The man at the car door clung for a moment; crumpled quite slowly to the ground.

'Bloody hooray,' said Rosher.

'Blonde or brunette?' smiled Mr Croker.

The sergeant half lowered the glasses, blinking against the glare they had gathered from the sun. In the authentic voice of Old Blubbergut he barked: 'There's something funny going on down there.'

'One would not doubt it,' said Mr Croker. 'One never did believe they spend all their time lying in the sun. May one hope for a tiny peep?'

Rosher, if he still knew the man was there, ignored him. He was raising the glasses again. With powerful binoculars, once they are taken away from the subject there is a problem. So great is the degree of magnification that with the naked eye it is not easy to pick out points of reference to help in finding it again. By the time Rosher relocated, the man who jumped into the hedge was out of it and hovering over his still recumbent mate; whom he now picked up and dragged, and shoved somehow into the back of the car. This done, he went to the driver's seat, made a futile effort to close the (presumably) mangled door, failed, and drove up the lane with it stuck open, to where there must have been an inlet to a field, or something. This enabled him to turn. He drove back to where the mannikin whose gun didn't seem to have helped him much lay unmoving where he had lain since he erupted out of the van. The driver got out; hovered; lifted the man from behind the shoulders and hauled him to the car.

Rosher lowered the glasses; thrust them upon Mr Croker. 'Car down there—watch it. Middle distance— twelve o'clock—line of bushy-topped trees.' He must get to the police car, radio the station. If a mobile patrol was handy it could block that lane. If one was not, an EMTAD—which means, translated from the jargon, Emergency To All Districts—should bring in a car with a mangled door, probably a scagged and battered side, certainly two lolling herberts in the back.

'What? What?' said Mr Croker.

'For Christ's sake!' said Sergent Rosher, all his joviality gone. 'Wake your bloody ideas up. I want to know where it goes.'

'I fail to understand,' said Mr Croker with affronted dignity.

'Middle distance—twelve o'clock—line of bushy-topped trees—'

'One has not the faintest idea what you are talking about.' No blame to Mr Croker. Army terms of reference are so much gibberish to anybody who managed to dodge even National Service. Especially when suddenly barked.

The American was coming back, stepping over the rock-strewn turf with the lightsome step and happy beam of the photographic buff who has it in the bag. These'd be worth blowing up big, hanging on the walls back home. 'This is really something,' he said. 'Hey—England's bigger than you thought it was, when you see it from up here.' But all cut up on a small scale, little bitty fields and things. No wide open spaces. And all smelling of damp grass.

The white beam jolted a bit as Rosher thrust the glasses urgently at him, barking: 'Take these. Down there—by a line of trees—a car. Oh sod it—never mind.' He turned and half ran towards the road.

'What's—er—?' the young man said. Disconcerting, sudden transmogrification of a jolly ape into an aggressive one.

'Something he saw, I believe,' Mr Croker explained. 'Strange character. Almost primitive. Many policemen are, of course. Necessarily, in a way—it shields them against intellectual querying of the status quo . . .' While he was speaking he turned and walked back towards the car. The American went with him.

Sergeant Rosher was already barking into the radio set, outlining what he had seen. The other men listened with a great interest. He concluded: 'If you move it, you can block 'em in the lane. No—they'll be out of it by now. Couple of cars—on the main road—'

The dehumanized small voice interrupted unemotionally through a crackle of static. 'Map reference?'

'Oh. Hang on.' Big, hairy hands fumbled among

papers in the glove compartment. 'Sod it,' said Sergeant Rosher, aside; and into the microphone: 'I've only got a tourist map. It doesn't show the lanes.'

'Ah,' said the voice, showing Lilliputian disapproval. 'Doesn't help much, does it? Big area. Lots of lanes.'

'Sod the lanes. Get 'em on to the main road.'

'Going which way?'

'How the bloody hell do I know? Block your end—buzz the city, block that end. Get an EMTAD out.'

'We'll do our best.' The voice sounded vaguely weary. Metal fatigue?

'Anybody wants to know, I'm going down for a shufti.' The sergeant jettisoned the microphone; scrambled across to the driving seat. 'Get in,' he snapped, and twisted the ignition key.

Clearly, this was no time to ask questions. Into the back went Mr Croker, into the passenger's seat came Patrolman Hopper. Almost before the doors slammed Sergeant Rosher had banged the gear lever into reverse, let in the clutch and shot off backward, loose scree skreeking under the tyres as he made space to turn in the narrow lane.

It is a characteristic of boulder-strewn places that some of the rocks become hidden under coarse grass and the bilberry bushes that flourish in such areas. Came a thump and a lurch. Sergeant Rosher growled 'Sod it' and shoved the gear lever, treading heavy. The car shot forward; shrieked through its sharp turn and took to the road. A hundred yards on it stopped, the engine sputtering to silence.

'What the bloody hell,' snarled the sergeant, making the starter motor whine.

Patrolman Hopper had poked his head out from the open window, looking back along the way they had come. 'We're leaving a trail,' he said, 'and there's helluva smell of gas. Guess we knocked a hole in the tank.' The tactful guest uses the plural to include himself in cock-up.

'Fuck, fuck, fuck it,' said Sergeant Rosher.

Mr Croker spoke now, from the back. 'Well—one must say, you gentlemen certainly see life. I should think the ratepayers will be very happy, the price of the stuff nowadays.'

'You shut your trap,' the sergeant barked, and reached across for the radio mike. He'd have to raise the station again to report the situation. Embarrassing—people would titter. But sod it—they couldn't all walk home, somebody would have to come and pick them up.

Patrolman Hopper, tactful man, kept silence, mulling over a new discovery. Fuck it, the ape-man said when he got riled, just like the fellows at home. Perhaps they all did, these stiff-lipped, withdrawn and oddly alien characters who had been determinedly smiling since he arrived, and uttering, in English all right but a funny sort of English, little jokes most of which he didn't get. Well, well, well. Maybe they were brothers after all, under the skin. The apeman at least was human.

It was getting late when Gaylord Hopper entered the Albion Hotel, where he was staying with his wife. A small hotel—there are no big ones in the town—but comfortable, in a brownly Victorian way, and very interesting. Tonight, for instance, when he came through an old revolving door into the strangely muted reception hall— feet on the brown carpet made no sound, and all the colours seemed to fade into brown—behind the brown desk stood the character called Phillips, in a brown and brass-buttoned uniform. He was old enough to wear a plethora of wrinkles, pink as if he lived on shrimp cocktails, and he made curious little bows like an ancient clockwork toy. Everything here felt old, but not seedy. Phillips made his little bow and said, in soft and kind of upper-crust tones: 'Good night, sir.'

'Good night.' The young man had heard Britons—

mostly old ones, those who stayed in this hotel—respond quite pleasantly with 'Good night, Phillips;' but this casual tossing around of class distinction he could not himself manage. On his first two evenings he had responded in kind, returning good night sir with good night sir; but this, he gathered, was never done. So now he simply said good night, smiling broadly to tell the pink man that no offence was intended, but he just couldn't manage Phillips. Not like that, in cold blood out of the blue.

He entered the antique elevator (wrought-iron gates, mahogany bodywork) and pulled on the rope. The contraption ascended sedately, to decant him two floors up. Only attics and the roof above this. Apart from two new apartment blocks rising too many stories (the British quaintly called them skyscraper blocks) all the buildings in the town were squatty, and most of them seemed to be old. A faint redolence of floor polish hung on the air as he walked along the carpeted, hushed corridor to the suite hired for him, presumably by the ratepayers.

His wife was home. No doubt about that. Not in the big and brownish living-room set with heavy, unexpectedly comfortable furniture; but when he entered her voice came from the bedroom beyond, slurred a little at the edges.

'Where the hell have you been?'

Always, at her bad times, coming home brought a tightness to his gut. He felt his stomach clench as he walked across the living-room. 'Working. Went out to bring a feller in—car broke down on the way back.'

'Working. That's my boy. All the time working—that's my boy.' She lay on the old-fashioned bed in her nightgown, the one that clung to breasts and nipples and all the soft curves of her body. When she walked in it—wow! Beside her, on the bedside table, the depleted bottle and half-filled glass.

'It's what I'm here for,' he said. 'It's what they pay me for. Remember?'

'It's what I'm here for, it's what I'm here for.' She mimicked him in a parrot-like voice. Sat up. Her lovely breasts altered shape, softly quivering as they re-settled. Those breasts, he had admitted to himself in his solitary soul-searching, had been one of the more potent factors that led him to marriage. Not that marriage had been necessary to their enjoyment; but he knew that if others had not enjoyed—or were not enjoying—them too, plenty would like nothing better. He had wanted them all to himself. And he'd thought he loved her. The hell of it was: beyond desire, he found he did. Now he stated the very obvious.

'You've been drinking.'

'I haven't been drinking,' she said. 'I *am* drinking.' To prove it she reached for the glass. Swallowed whisky. Focused upon him the huge, brilliantly beautiful dark eyes that came with her Italian ancestry. 'What the hell else is there to do in this dead dump?'

'Oh, honey,' he said. 'For Chrissakes!'

'Never mind about Christ's sake.' Her voice, lowish in pitch and full-toned when she was sober, took on aggressive shrillness when drunk. 'What about me, cooped up in this morgue with a bunch of corpses?'

'If you'd only get out and meet them a bit, they're not so bad—'

'Meet 'em? I've met enough of 'em. I met the mayor, and the lady mayor, and half the goddam police. I met 'em at the airport and I met 'em at the reception and I met 'em when the lady mayor came and took me in her snooty Rolls-Royce, all around the women's clubs. I've seen all I want to see. Stand-off bastards.'

'They're not so bad—a lot of 'em are fine, when you get to know them—'

'*You* get to know them, then. You love 'em so much,

you get to know them. Don't mind me—you have fun.'
She swigged again at her glass.

It wasn't the British. Whenever the thing came on her,
she said much the same about the people back home. The
pattern of it was familiar. He said: 'Shall we keep the
voice down? There's folks next door—'

'Folks? There's no folks here—they're all corpses.' The
black eyes glared at him. 'Shit on you,' she said. 'Mr
Fucking Hopper—shit on you.' And she burst into tears.

He crossed to the bed; lay beside her, taking her in his
arms. 'Honey—honey,' he crooned. 'Come on now,
honey.' She clutched him, her face burying in the hollow
between his shoulder and neck. 'Oh Christ,' she wept. 'Oh
Christ, oh Christ, oh Christ.'

CHAPTER 3

It had been another late night for Rosher. Dark was down
before a patrol car became free to pick up young Hopper
and Mr Croker, who was openly relishing the situation.
The sergeant himself stayed with the damaged vehicle,
awaiting a tow-truck, which dropped him off eventually
at the station.

By now it was midnight; and he still had things to do.
The booking in of Croker and a written report of his
arrest; a second report, setting out in full the incident
seen from the hill; yet another, detailing damage (so far
as known) to an official car and the way it happened—it
all took time. He replaced the cover on the hated typewriter at half past one, a clear and starry morning. That
finished the statutory chores.

But even now he did not go home. No senior rank on
duty, ordering him to stay, because even police stations
run down a little in the small hours of Sunday; but the top

brass on standby (if you except the Chief Constable, who
has the ultimate can heavy upon his shoulder and so is
never really off duty) was Detective Chief Superintendent
(Percy) Fillimore; and that man was Detective-Sergeant
Rosher's implacable foe.

Without doubt the blower had given Percy the gist of
Rosher's strange story. How could it be otherwise? This is
the very reason why senior men are turn-and-turn-about
on standby—so that when the station gathers in matter
outrageous beyond the normal pub punch-ups, petty
larcenies, pissed-up motorists careering into stone walls,
and men driven desperate by the horrors of domesticity
beating hell out of the wife and nippers, the can may be
passed forthwith legitimately upward. Failure to do so
saddles the omitter with a can of his own devising.

So without doubt, Percy knew. Probably, he also knew
that the car had met mishap. Certainly it was he who
directed the diversion of two more patrol cars to peer nar-
rowly up and down the lanes in the salient area. Of these,
there are not a few. A veritable network, it is. Nobody
thought to rush an Ordnance Survey map up to Rosher
on the hill, to pinpoint the position there and then with
all the landmarks spread out for easy checking. By the
time he got to one at the station where pinpointing was
not so damned easy, the cars were already burning up the
world's oil reserves, wild-goosing around the countryside.
More use they'd have been to the community parked
around unobtrusive corners, fingering breathalysers close
by the places where men drink.

Soon after restless Rosher arrived in the radio room to
hear the incoming calls, one of the cars spoke, saying: 'It's
a bit bloody stupid, Eric—all we can see is what the
headlights pick up. We don't even know what we're looking for, really, do we? Over.'

'All right, Ted,' said the uniform sergeant handling
this end. 'I'll get on to the brass, see about knocking it off

until the morning. Over.'

'Makes sense to me,' the cruising car replied. 'Nobody's going to just dump a car with a couple of stiffs in it, are they? Not in a lane. If they have, it's not on our beat. Over and out.'

The uniform sergeant picked up a telephone. Began to dial. Rosher said: 'Haven't got the car yet, then?'

'Nope. Nary a sign of it. Couple of dented jalopies stopped on the main road, but there's a lot of it about. It's the bloody metal they use nowadays, lean on 'em and they crumple.' He turned his attention to the telephone. 'We've got problems here,' he told it. No deferential sir, no name, no title given to whoever was at the other end. 'The lads can't see a thing. Moon's down—not much light under trees and bushes.' He listened a moment to a little squawking. 'Yep—yeah, that's what I was thinking. Call 'em off—put 'em back on at dawn. It's only a couple of hours. Right.' He hung up. Some policemen never do learn that respect should be proffered to senior rank. Especially at two in the morning.

'Percy?' said Rosher.

'Yep. All off till the morning. Oh yeah—it's your little lark, ain't it? Well, I've got to say this—you've whiled away a long and tedious night.' Thick fingers clicked switches to contact the cruising patrols.

Rosher walked away. He went home to his lonely, increasingly cluttered and dusty house on a hill, where he sat awhile in his armchair and then lay awhile on the bed, fully dressed apart from his durable jacket. This he took off, replacing it with his dressing-gown before he lay down. He would nap for an hour. No more. Then on with his coat, and out into the dawn.

Not a wink did he sleep. It capered in his mind that he did not come well out of the night's events. In the hands of ill-disposed Percy it could all warp quite easily. Not only was he on a deviation from the direct route that should have led Henry Croker to the cell, but of the three men present, only he saw the happening. And he'd had no map to pin location, the patrol cars were put into action entirely upon his unsupported word that somewhere down there something funny had taken place. And then—how for Christ's sake had he managed to do it? He didn't normally flap like a bloody rookie—he'd knocked a hole in a CID car.

Yes. Sod it. Yes—Percy would quite enjoy this. And the Old Man would hear of it—the skinny-gutted bastard would make sure of that. Right now, with promotion delicately poised, as it were, Rosher did not need this. It came between him and a little nap. Instead of sleeping, he lay fretting and fuming. If that twat of a Yank hadn't shoved field glasses at him, he need never have seen a thing.

At the end of his hour he rose, to splash cold water over himself. He shaved, using his electric razor for speed rather than the old soap-and-safety method which he preferred. By now the kettle was boiling. He made tea; let it brew while he found a clean shirt—he had certain domestic systems reasonably worked out—and came back to hack, butter and smear with gooseberry jam (he was out of marmalade again, sod it) a hunk of bread. Only now did he pour the tea, grown beetle-black and biting, the way he liked it. He stood in the kitchen where brown rings and blobs of grey fat tended to congregate on working surfaces, and munched up his breakfast with his brown teeth. He then made a little water, shrugged into his jacket, settled his black hat low upon his brow, draped his battleship grey raincoat over his arm because you never know, in England, and stepped out into the new day.

A beautiful day, but he gained no true benefit from it. Too much on his mind, and he'd seen a lot of dawns. He piloted his ageing car down his hill and across the deserted town, fresh as though newly aerosoled. When he got to the station, Detective Chief Superintendent (Percy) Fillimore was already there. He emerged from his office as the sergeant came clacking down the corridor; and he said: 'Well, Sergeant Rosher—here's a funny business.'

Here is the reason why Percy was at the station soon after dawn on a Sunday morning: he was a terminal worrier. They rang him last night to pass on Rosher's story, and at once his antenna shot up. Anybody but Rosher, the facts outlined would have brought worry, yes—all looming work did, as every appearance knots the gut of the good actor—but it would have been the familiar fret that borders and blends with curiosity. This blend makes good coppers; and nobody could deny that Percy was a good copper. But: This was Rosher; and every bloody time, it seemed, that he got tangled with Rosher, somebody fell headlong into the fragrant pile. He'd had to dance a tricky little hornpipe at the time when Rosher himself dived in, to avoid being spattered. It was—and he sensed this—extremely difficult for calamity of some sort not to precipitate, when they came together. Nature had so formed them as to create the perfect personality clash; so that they worked, not in harness, but tugging violently against each other.

When he got the phone call last evening, and learned that Rosher was at it again, instinct said take cover. But this he could not do, being the brass on standby. So he ordered the cars out and in time went to bed. Came a second call, in the small hours. He suspended action until dawn and plumped up his pillow. But no sleep came. He lay beside his lightly snoring wife, fretting in his bed as Rosher fretted.

If this thing blew up—and things involving Rosher had a way of magnifying—it wouldn't look good, his lying here while God knew what was happening on his manor. Three men in a bashed-up car, vanished. And two of them might be—dead? Murdered?

If there was a car. If there were any men.

One thing, for sure: there was a Rosher.

Before dawn he was up. As the first streak touched the sky he tiptoed out of the house and freewheeled his car down the sloping drive to avoid waking his wife who would sniff for a week if he did. Better be down there, physically on the spot and in command. Take no chances.

Now he came out from his office; and there was Rosher, clacking square-toed in his durable suit and that stupid bloody hat, like a ponced-up shop-steward gorilla on his way to a Zoo Workers' Union meeting.

He said: 'Well, Sergeant Rosher—here's a funny business.'

'Uh-huh,' said Rosher. Stern-faced, and his hard little eyes glittering.

'A very funny business.' Percy's own eyes—narrow eyes, set in a narrow head just a smidgin too small for a narrow body—exuded no bonhomie. He reopened the door which he had just closed. 'Step in for a moment, will you?' Back he went, into the office. Rosher trod in behind him. 'I have your written report here,' said Percy.

'Uh-huh.' The guarded semi-grunt again, giving nothing away.

'What I do not understand—among other things,' Percy said, 'is what you were doing on top of Deacon Hill.'

'Watching the sunset.'

Don't try that barking tone on me, you bastard, said the brain in Percy's head; but on the outside, only his eyebrows rose. His mouth said, as if his ears mistook: 'The *sunset?*'

'I had the Yank with me. It's one of the sights.'

'I am to understand you were gadding about on a sight-seeing tour? In an official car? In spite of orders to conserve fuel? With an arrested criminal in the back?'

'Mr Hopper was given into my charge. I understood I

was expected to treat him as a guest.'

'Mr *O*'Hopper is here to study our methods. Country jaunts do not come within the scope of our brief. Sightseeing tours are being arranged, I believe, by the town council. For him *and* his wife. It is not for us to usurp the privilege.'

'We were on official business. My instructions were to take him with me on the arrest.'

'Would you perhaps agree that you exceeded your instructions in gallivanting him up Deacon Hill in company with an habitual criminal?'

Don't bang him. Don't bang him. Think of the pension. 'No specific orders were given.'

'There is a standing order, Sergeant, augmented by one recently introduced. Mobile personnel will not deviate from the most direct route to and from their destination, and if forced to do so will immediately inform this station, by means of radio communication. The other is: petrol will at all times be conserved, by every possible means.'

'It's no further, across country.'

'It is two miles further.' Already Percy had been doing homework. 'To say nothing of grinding up and down in low gear. You appear also to have damaged a valuable CID car.'

Here, he raised his narrow shoulders, bracing himself as every wise man did when the sergeant brought out his great handkerchief. Rosher blew the trump that rattled windows and (could it be true? A Constable Basil Humner swore it was. Said he'd seen it) flaked down plaster from walls; wiped; tucked the sheet away and removed that black hat to scratch the ten-penny tonsure on the crown of his cannonball head; coughed, and said: 'Hrrrmph.'

Percy resumed. 'These matters, of course, will be subject to fuller investigation at a later date. No doubt under the direct jurisdiction of the Chief Constable. Let us turn

now to your report. Perhaps you will be so good as to des-
cribe again the incident you allege so fortuitously seeing
from the hill.'

'It's all in my written report.'

'I would prefer to have it verbally.'

Rosher spoke, at no great length. When he finished,
Percy said: 'Two other men were with you. I take it they
will corroborate?'

'They didn't see it. I had the glasses.'

'It did not occur to you to hand them over? To secure
witnesses?' Surely, the high-arched eyebrows said, you
could not be such a clown?

Hammer his choppers down his throat.

No—no—the pension. Cling. Cling to the hope of
salvation, of resurrection back to inspector status.

'It was happening too fast. Takes time, to point out a
subject. The other man has to find it and refocus.' What
a thick voice came out of the sergeant. And a small vein
pulsed visibly in his forehead.

'I am familiar, Sergeant,' said the Chief Superintendent, 'with the techniques pertaining to field glasses.'

But never, Rosher told him savagely inside his head, in
the field. If you copped war glasses at all, it would have
been to see who was helping himself to ordnance stores,
fifty miles behind the lines.

Percy was speaking again. 'I must say, Mr Rosher, I
find the entire episode surprising. Disturbing. From a
man of your experience, one would have expected a different mode of conduct. However. No doubt all this will
be gone into later. I am assuming rightly, I take it? Your
presence here at this time is due to an intention to inspect
these lanes?' Truly, a needling policeman, if he has a
reasonable vocabulary, can give pointers in pomposity
even to striking Trades Union leaders, right across the
board and at the grass roots.

'I thought I might. Yes.'

'Then I suggest you join one of the other cars. We don't want any more accidents.'

There sprang to Rosher's lips a snarling retort that he would use his own car; but he was a man of notably parsimonious habit, a cruiser downhill even before the OPEC men started their jolly capers. And hot-headed attack, Percy holding such inflatable cards, could put heavy mockers on. Wherefore he bit back hard, producing the sound, 'Herrr-grmph.'

Percy turned away, heading for the window; where he would stand with his hands behind him, looking out. 'That will be all, Mr Rosher,' he said.

'Hrrmph,' said Rosher, and tramped away fuming. When he reached the CID room he was constrained to whip out his great handkerchief and to go through his ritual again. The room being empty at this early Sunday hour, it gave back interesting reverberations. Even the bum-scratching with which he oftimes concluded, in private or the company of men well known, gave forth gritty sound as the nails ran over the durable serge. They just don't make stuff like that any more.

Two cars were gone already. One was just leaving. He entered it and shot away in company with Constable John Bingham, 23, and Constable Kevin Crabbe, 24. Both much too young for him. Ridiculous, how young the police were getting nowadays. He sat glum in the back of the garish blue-and-white painted vehicle while they talked together of discos, crumpet, football and crumpet, touching only lightly upon cricket, currently in full season, and not at all upon boxing. After an initial approach which he discouraged with a grunt, they left him alone, with relief. If the old sod wanted to sit glowering out of the window—okay, that was his problem. You couldn't blame him, really—at that age what have you got to live for?

They found nothing.

Young Gaylord Hopper was up and out early, walking in the town. Not crack of dawn, as were Percy and Rosher; but soon after six o'clock he came through the brown hotel hall, where nobody seemed to be on duty, and drew the bolt that released from set position the old revolving door. He stepped into a street bland with early sun and Sunday hush, but smelling peculiarly damp. England always did. It was not shrouded perpetually in pea-soup fog, as he had expected, nor did it rain all the time, as he had been given to understand it would. On the contrary, for most of the week since they arrived the sun had beamed from a wonderful sort of misty blue sky. Nevertheless, it smelled a little damp. So did the people, in their woolly jackets called cardigans, their boob-hugging jumpers and funny sort of bank-tellers' suits.

He rather liked it all. Took a little getting used to; but he liked all these old houses with crusty walls and little windows, he liked the old, old parish church, he enjoyed the inconvenient Victorian-built rabbit-warren police station, he even liked the people—nearly all tucked up in bed right now, thousands and thousands of them, all lying prone. Well, he was a young man with a gift for liking people. He walked through the town now, his the only footsteps stirring sound between quietly receptive walls. Think of all those people, lying prone. Only ones upright—the oddball, the fisherman, people like the police with duties to rouse them out: and people like himself, having problems.

He came back into the hotel, pain and fret and all, shortly before eight. By now the day porter was on duty—another old character, much younger than he who bowed like clockwork, but without hair and with the thick brogue of a part of the country called Norwich, a long way from here. He said he was from Norwich, when Gaylord asked. Pronounced it Norridge, so it took a little tracking on the map. This morning he was reading the

Sunday papers, behind the brown desk upon which stood neat little piles of them, for convenient purchase by guests.

He said, very pleasantly: 'Ar—good mornun, Mester O'Hubber. Bun owt, hev 'ee? Oi wooneered oo undone ole bolt.'

Hopper's acclimatizing ear made a free translation. ' 'Morning,' he said, beaming widely to show he meant no evil. 'Yeah—just been for a walk around. Papers, huh? Guess I'd better take a few up with me.'

As he gathered papers, the porter said: 'Doon s'poose yew'm be untrusted in cruckit, being Amurican, loike?'

'Er—not really, no.' He'd seen one game—part of a game—of cricket. Couldn't make head or tail of it, but it seemed very slow.

'Wooden worry ee, then, wud ut, England with their baaacks to the wall?' The man grinned. Good grey eyes, but yellowish, uneven teeth. The British were not very strong on teeth. 'Doan worry me, arl that much.'

Not at all sure what this was all about—certain dialect pronunciations foxed him still—the young man broadened his white grin and said as he paid for the papers: 'Bully for you.'

The porter accepted his coins; said: 'Maanaage our mooney all roight, yew Amurican gennelmen, since us went decimal. Used to get in a roight ole two-and-eight, soome on 'em, in the old powns, shulluns and pence days.'

'D'you get many Americans staying here?'

'Not what yew'd call many, noo. Drop in now n agin, see ole town and stop oover-noight.'

'Ah,' said young Hopper. 'Well—thanks.' He turned away to the antiquated elevator. Watching him go, the porter thought, probably in his own dialect but a man is so used to his inner thinking he does not register the shape of it: wonder if he pisses it up the way his wife does? Looks fresh enough. Nice-looking piece, she is. Wouldn't mind giving her a rub of the brush. Although they reckon American women are all frigid. He returned to his Sunday treat of sex by proxy, courtesy of the *News of the World*.

Young Hopper entered that mahogany-bound elevator, which bore a strange, hand-lettered plea thumbtacked to the wall. Guests are requested, it said, not to stand under the lift. He pulled the starting cord, wondering as he had wondered for a week what the hell that meant. Did they tend, for some peculiarly British reason, to gather at the bottom of the shaft? The aged structure shook itself a little, and carried him accurately enough to the desired floor. It could hardly do otherwise, unless it suddenly went berserk and shot screaming through the roof. He walked the muffling brown carpet soundlessly to his door.

She was still in bed; but not asleep, as she had been when he slipped away. Drink will put you out like a light, but wake-up comes early. He tossed the papers on to the bed. 'Hi,' he said. 'Read all about it.'

'Where you been?' she asked. Not the strident demand of last night, but the sick, almost dazed query of fragile morning after.

'Just out. Nowhere in particular. Around the town.'

'You sure start fast,' she said. No hostility in it. Thank God, there was no hostility in it.

'It's a beautiful morning.'

'It's a helluva morning.' She raised both hands, pressing the heels against her eyes. The movement showed the beauty of her slim arms and shoulders, the bedclothes sliding down revealed her lovely breasts, naked since she suddenly wanted him—it—after—during—her weeping last night.

He said no more. Went into the bathroom and returned with aspirin, and a glass of water. She was sitting up now, a pillow shoved into position behind her back to support her. Slim, virginal, very young she looked, those heart-stopping breasts full and firm, bigger than one would have expected on so slight a frame. He proffered the glass and the small white tablets. 'What I need,' she said, 'is a hair of the dog.'

He kept his white smile screwed firmly into position. 'What you need,' he told her, playing it light, 'is aspirin and a good kick in the ass.' It wasn't over yet. Until it was—a day, two days, a week; it might be more—you had to be careful. She could be quick to take offence.

Today she reacted meekly, taking the tablets and the glass from his outstretched hands. 'Just don't climb on my back, will you?' she said; popped the aspirin into her mouth; followed up with the water and swallowed. Her breasts quivered, subtly recontouring to differing tensions. She handed back the glass; sat for a moment in silence while he found a place for it on the bedside table. Then she said: 'What are you doing today?'

'Not entirely sure,' he said. 'There's an old guy called Rosher [he still made it sound like Russia], I was with him yesterday. He said to come in around two o'clock, but I'm not sure he realized it'd be Sunday. He was pretty het up—he'd just made a hole in the car.'

She did not ask how he came to do that, or remark on the oddity of a detective called Russia who didn't even know what day it was. She showed no interest at all. What she said was: 'If you're free until two, you could come back to bed.'

'They'll be serving breakfast—'

'Come back to bed.' She pushed the bedclothes down to her thighs with one hand. The other cupped her vulva, middle finger moving slightly.

Immediately, as always, he felt his body respond. 'Sure,' he said. 'Okay. Sure.' He began to remove his clothes.

Afterwards she said: 'Good?'

'Good.' And it was. But not so good as last night. It was a secret shame in him that the acme of their sexual congress came when she was drunk, demanding his body, treating his genitals brutally with teeth and nails; joining him to her with urgent hands, to writhe and gasp and thrust moaningly under him until both collapsed into obliterating orgasm.

In self-analysis, he wondered if the irresistible force of desire that swept him when she was drunk stemmed from the stress of it — the body uses sex as a soporific in times of stress — or was engendered by her orgiastic abandon when alcohol liberated her from structured inhibition; or whether he was some kind of pervert, able to attain full satisfaction only when the woman was out of kink, or utterly helpless. Because he had taken her more than once when she was flopping like a warm doll, completely passed out; impelled by supra-normal hunger that increased as he undressed her for bed, and peaked when she lay naked and unconscious, flavouring the air with liquor fume as she breathed, roseated breasts moving, the pink petals of her femininity moist and visible, unguarded under the soft hair.

This morning, as always when they both were sober, was good but not all that good. He lay beside her and knew that she had not come. When she did, she swooned; and sometimes sexual release broke the 'attack' that had her drinking. Today there was no relaxation in her. He lay quietly, pretending to have drifted into sleep; and after a while he knew her fingers were moving, until her breath snagged and jagged secretly and the bed moved to her rigidly controlled lurching. After that, she lay still.

He missed breakfast; but by lunch-time he was in the dining-room, eating alone. Around him people demolished — soberly, as the British do in public, and if they were married couples not talking at all — roast beef with the traditional Yorkshire pudding and mounds of vegetables, or whatever equivalent their long brain-washed stomachs demanded for suitable distension at Sunday lunch; but he took grapefruit, an omelette with salad on the side, a helping of very good apple pie and a cup of atrocious coffee. Finding it satisfying, if not stimulating, he had a duplicate meal set out and sent up to her on a tray. Then he sat for a while, smoking the first of his three-a-day cigars.

Still in the rumpled bed, she had not touched the food when he came back to the bedroom, but she was working on the coffee; the uptilted cup hiding her nose as he entered. Lovely, the movement of her delicate throat and the unblemished underside of her chin. She lowered the cup, making an exaggerated shudder that showed in hunched up shoulders, slim arms, vibration of breasts. 'What in hell,' she wondered, 'do they make it with?'

'I think they mix it with old cold tea-bags,' he said. 'Something to do with the economic situation. You ought to eat something.'

'I'm not hungry. I'll grab something later.'

He didn't press. She would eat or she would not, which-ever way suited her. Anyway, they'd be feeding her tonight. 'How are you feeling?' he asked.

'Rough.' She smiled at him suddenly. Incredible, how young and untouched she looked, when her great dark eyes smiled and the dimples appeared, and the perfect teeth gleamed. 'Lot better, though. That's what you do for me, you and your randy old cock.'

'Talking of randy—who started it?' Nice of you, honey—but if sex has soothed you, it came out of your fingers. He glanced at the clock on the bedside table. Nice room, this, in spite of the brown overtones. Nice clock, thrown in with the rent. 'Well—I'd better be off. Old guy said two, it'll be past that by the time I get there. Rest easy, sweetheart.' He kissed her—still the scent of liquor clinging—and fondled her breasts for a moment, teasing the nipples erect. Kissed her again and headed for the door; paused on the way out to say: 'Hey—don't forget they're coming for us around seven, will you?'

'I won't,' she said.

'I'll be back.' He winked, and was gone.

Sergeant Rosher knew damn well, there *must* be spoor in one of those lanes. The crews in the cars were not peering closely enough, that was all. And this was hardly to their discredit, he had to admit it. Even now they had no sure map reference, and no clear idea of what they were looking for. Most of them did not even know the area well enough to travel it without an Ordnance Survey sheet spread on the passenger's knee; and when the driver is focused mainly on narrow road and hedge-blind bends, and half his oppo's attention on keeping check on location and direction, observation is not all that it might be. As yet, there was not enough substance in the situation to justify squads of footmen scouring, all on Sunday overtime. Wherefore, sign—he knew it must be so, whatever anybody else thought—was being overlooked.

He did all the sensible things. He had his crew run him to the top of Deacon Hill, where he stood with the map and worked out exactly where it had to be. He had then radioed a definite reference back to the station, and taking command of the car he was travelling in, directed it to the spot. In time they were joined by the three other engaged patrols, and a certain amount of foot-searching took place.

Nothing turned up. They all left the area around 10.30 a.m. It costs money to keep four cars cruising, and leaves gaps in the ranks where they should be on normal duty. If you decide to leave the regular duty patrols undisturbed and call in off-duty cews—this costs more money. Rate-payers' money. The canny commanders balance factors, and play it as the ear suggests.

Detective Chief Superintendent (Percy) Fillimore was still in the station when Rosher arrived back shortly before eleven, but the two men did not meet again. Percy remained shut away behind the closed door of his office; and Rosher, after sticking around for a time in hope that an incoming radio call from some unspecified duty car would announce the discovery of a bashed-up vehicle with bodies or a dinted motor-caravan, went home.

He lunched alone. Not too badly, because by now his culinary spasms took him beyond the frying-pan; but troubled in his mind, all the good humour of yesterday evaporated. His bloody luck, copping Percy for the brass on standby. The bastard would do what had to be done—but something always went up the stick when he got near Percy. Take this morning already. There'd nearly been a fist in Percy's eye. Clobber a brass-bound bastard on a Sunday morning and where are you, in the delicately balanced promotion stakes? Promotion? Lucky, in this case, if you didn't go down—and out.

A lamb chop is what he ate, with boiled potatoes and peas from a tin. Canned fruit and custard (also out of a can) to follow. For all the treat he got out of it, he might as well have opened another of his many tins of beans. And he'd forgotten to buy cheese again, so fuck it. He washed up at once, having learned well the depressing properties of a greasy sink filled with a growing mountain of cold, fat-congealed crockery. This done, he sat for ten minutes where every man must sit daily, given a reasonably active bowel, his eyes upon a newspaper but his mind elsewhere. And then he sought his black hat and drove again to the station, arriving there five minutes before the visiting Yank arrived.

Sergeant Barney Dancey, working the dayshift, was on duty behind the enquiry desk when young Hopper came in. He looked up from what he was writing and said: 'Hallo, young feller-me-lad. What're you doing here?

Don't you get a rest day in the States?'

The almost too eager, too white teeth beamed forth. 'Hi, Sarge. Sergeant Russia said to come in around two o'clock.'

'What a way to spend a honeymoon.'

'It was this, or Niagara Falls.' The town newspapers had made much of the honeymoon angle; as had the Chief, back home. 'It'll make a great trip for you, son,' he'd said. 'Honeymoon in Europe, all expenses paid.'

Sergeant Barney was grinning. 'What's wrong with Niagara Falls?'

'See one waterfall, you've seen 'em all.' It wasn't really their honeymoon, of course. They'd spent that in Arkansas, three months ago. Why Arkansas? Her people lived there, and she wanted him to meet them.

The sergeant laughed. He liked this young man. Mind you, challenge and he would have to cogitate long before naming somebody he did not like. 'You'll find him inside, somewhere. Don't let him come between you and your nearest and dearest.'

'Sure.' The lad moved on, thinking: if you only knew it, it doesn't need a big ape or anybody else. There's something bigger than that between us, and it's all rooted in her. Or in me? Or in both of us? One thing's for sure: the honeymoon's over. And if I hadn't managed to keep it dark, what I know about her now, I'd have been passed over for this trip. 'Remember, son—you ain't just a cop. You go as an ambassador . . .'

Maybe it would have been better. She doesn't like it here.

Who was it said you never know a person until you live with them?

Everybody did.

I ought to stay there with her.

Well, you can't. And that's that.

He found Rosher in the CID room, only man there,

and was struck afresh by the peculiarly gorilla construction of him. The forehead, the shape of the nose and the eyes in particular; the barrel body and the unexpectedly short and bandy legs giving the impression of a waggle-bummed walk with big, hairy hands dangling down around the knees. At home, one or two of the old guys hanging on for retirement worked in suits; but no suit ever came his way so thick and obviously without built-in obsolescence. And who else, for Chrissake, ever wore such a hat? He had it on now, reading through an official paper of some sort over by one of the desks. The young man said: 'Hi, Al.'

The gorilla-man looked up. His eyes had a hard look. You wouldn't have called them melting yesterday. Today they had a hard look. 'Hrrmph,' he said. 'Yes. You, is it? I'm not officially here.'

'Ah,' said Patrolman Hopper. 'You said to meet you here at two o'clock.'

'Ah,' said Rosher. 'Uh-huh. Well—mm.' His eyes moved back to the typewritten form.

Okay, okay, young Hopper thought. So you don't want to play. I can always go home, coming in was your idea.

Rosher, too, had a brain in working order. About to embark on a private and quite unofficial inspection of that lane, all alone and with no prattling juveniles to distract him, his first reaction to Hopper's arrival was annoyance. Sod it—he'd done his stint of jolly host. But then he thought: witness. If you find something portable and bring it in, it's not beyond Percy to imply that you planted it.

He looked up, saying less brusquely: 'I'm going to take a look at that lane. You might as well come along.'

'Okay,' said Hopper. 'Sure.' His thinking went: I'd sooner go home, stay with her. But I can't say so. Nobody said anything about taking the day off. I'd have thought those lanes would have been well gone over already, at home we'd have saturated them by now. But keep buttoned up—you're a guest, and they have their own way of doing things. Perhaps they have been working at it—you've been out of touch since last evening.

The ape-man put his paper down. 'Right, then,' he said. 'Let's get weaving.' And he started for the door leading into the clacking passage. Hopper came behind. This time, the sergeant did not stand aside to yield precedence. In the soil of long habit, new courtesy finds small nourishment. He led on across the reception hall and again went first through the door into the street. He entered an ageing black car, slamming himself into the driver's seat. Hopper climbed in on the passenger's side. The sergeant said, 'Hang on a minute,' and got out again. Ape-walked back to the building, leaving his guest sitting there. He was about to bend rules, and one of the laws of survival is: if you don't know the oppo wished upon you, get shot of him while you do it.

Ten minutes passed before he returned. Hopper found a Sunday newspaper folded into the glove compartment, and passed the time with it. A vicar had run off with mother of five. Crime figures appalling, said police chief. Herbert Oliver Uppett was alleged to have cloven blonde, attractive divorcee Mrs Lilian Skinner (38) with a chopper. A knighted actor was charged with flashing—some are dogged by misfortune—to a Detective-Constable Derek Stringfold, who happened to stand next to him in a Leicester Square toilet. Told he would be arrested, he said: 'Why didn't you say you were a policeman?' and England had collapsed again.

The ape approached. As he inserted himself back behind the wheel, Patrolman Hopper refolded the newspaper—skinny, it was, compared with the block-busting Sunday wrist-sprainers of home; but what it lacked in volume it made up in sex—saying: 'Hope you don't mind me reading your paper.'

'Hmp,' said Rosher, who did not approve of anybody using anything owned by him without respectful request and guarded permission. He started the engine and let in the clutch. They moved off with a small shudder at just about the time when the Hon. David Lawney went in to bat on a very attractive cricket field not many miles away.

When they reached the lane—it had no name, but Rosher knew the way to it now—he tooled the car along easy, not expecting spoor this far on but meaning to miss nothing; until they came to the dog-leg bend, one of three but obviously the one he saw from the hill. Here they found a car drawn up and two men, one standing and the other squatted, closely inspecting the road surface. The standing man, seeing who had arrived, called over as they came out from their seats.

' 'Afternoon, Alf. Step wary—Ron reckons he's drawn blood.'

'Blood?' said Rosher.

'That's blood.' The squatting man nodded to dots on the roadway. He had done something with something from his little black bag, and it made the dots jump out from the surrounding ground. 'If I'm not wrong, and I bloody well am not, that's a patch of it, left of where you're standing.'

'Clever little bugger, isn't he?' said his oppo. ' 'Course, he went to night school.'

'Don't tramp about, gents,' the first man said, and went back to examination through a Sherlock Holmes magnifying glass and to doing his particular thing. Laymen titter when they see a detective with a magnifying glass, but you may believe that they have their uses.

Rosher and young Hopper stayed where they were. The standing man went to the parked car and radio-reported to headquarters. Nobody, not even the visiting American, needed to wonder what happened next. A lot of men and a sufficiency of equipment would converge upon this little lane.

In his office, Detective Chief Superintendent (Percy) Fillimore was already organizing it. He had taken his morning and afternoon pills, his tablet and two 5ml spoonsful of a white emulsion designed to cut the churning of stomachs such as his, which wobble under stress; for here was a man whose hobbies were golf and hypochondria. This churning interior came upon him always when he knew, by experience and instinct, that a case was going to blow up. He swallowed the emulsion as soon as the call came through and set about the task of organizing. At which, he excelled. He had cars and personnel on their way in very short order, and with them the small van that formed a travelling forensic department. That lane and the adjacent area would be fine-tooth combed.

He had just clicked the switch of the old-fashioned intercom machine that stood on his desk and was deciding that a trip down there would be best, to see for himself whatever might blow up even as it blew, when the thing buzzed at him. He reclicked the switch. 'Yes?'

'Nice one here, sir,' the talking box said. 'We've found that car. In the wood by Upton Richard. Two stiffs in it.'

'Thank you,' said Percy. 'Kindly notify the Chief Constable.' And his gut rushed about like a goldfish.

CHAPTER 4

There is this to be said for England: on the very fringes even of its most evil industrial cities, good country abounds. Try as he may and does, the Briton cannot totally eradicate it. Climate helps, of course. Abundant rain forms the mushy compost into which root those variegated, leafy trees and all that ever-green grass. Pros-

perous sheep wax fat and woolly in it, contented cows
mild of eye and habit stand swag-udder deep in daisies,
ruminating upon the good fortune that calved them here.

Centuries ago men invented a game in this land and
called it cricket. They play it still, in the teeth of bar-
barian mirth from lesser breeds without the law. Not
them exactly, but the current crop of snorting fast
bowlers, crafty spinners with a concealed googlie,
elegantly wristy batsmen and plain, straightforward clob-
berers. Who, having seen white flannels against green
grass and heard the clean tak of red ball against
margarine-yellow bat, can say they are wrong? Especially
when lush trees fringing the outfield whisper and the
shadows begin to lengthen, blue against green as evening
creeps on, and ten are needed for victory, and the only
man left to bat is that great, big, beetle-browed bastard
who bowled the bumpers.

It does not often happen, this flood of evening sun that
lifts the game into glory. Men who can spectate only on
Sunday have gone from boyhood into advanced old age
without seeing it. But it was happening today, not far
from Hutton Fellows, to the favoured who sat in deck-
chairs or on the benches along the front of the Victorian
gingerbread pavilion, or stood clad in white crying
howzat as the umpire's finger rose and the Hon. David
Lawney stepped away from the wicket on his way back to
the pavilion.

It was hot. It was beautiful. He had just scored eighty-
seven, elegantly stopping the rot that suddenly ate up the
earlier batting and setting his team on the path to probable victory. He raised his bat in modest acknowledge-
ment, applauded in with restrained clapping by watcher
and foeman alike. He was, at this moment, very nearly
happy.

People spoke to him as he went up the little steps into
the good cool of the pretty wooden building. 'Nice

knock,' they said, and 'Well done, David.' He made deprecating murmurs, smiling; tall, elegant and thirty-two years old. Somebody handed him a cup of tea. He set it on a trestle-table while he rid himself of pads, batting gloves, bat and the shaped metal protector without which a man can be reduced to a writhing, spewing wreck before a fast bowler can round on the umpire, roaring with baleful eye, hands thrown to high heaven. Then he picked up the tea, drained the cup, asked for a refill from the big enamel pot and took it out into the sunshine. Old Colonel Farjeon-Stevens sat on a bench level with the pavilion door immediately to the left as he came out. 'Beautiful knock, David,' he said. 'Beautiful.'

'Thank you, sir.' The young man sat down on the bench; sipped his tea.

'Need that, I dare say,' the old soldier said. 'Thirsty work, day like this. Reminded me of Dexter. At his best. Glorious.'

'Hardly in Dexter's class, sir, I'm afraid.' Charming smile the young man had, and from his chiselled mouth came the accent nurtured at Eton, buffed up at Oxford.

'I don't know, I don't know. Could be, if you took it seriously.' The Colonel shared the accent. He also wore a black patch, having lost one eye, not quite on the field of honour but by ham-fisted action of a swaddy in the Pay Corps, in which he had had the honour to serve. He was leaning over, on an inspection, to scrutinize a ledger, and the silly bugger, holding his pen vertical upon his desk the wrong way up, stuck the nib right in it.

'More important things to do, sir.'

'Nothing more important than cricket, my boy. Nothing.' To your fanatic, this is true. The Colonel was one; so much so that he laid aside his bottle all through the season, in the interest of clear sight and concentration. From September until late April he tippled the cricketless time away, viewing the world (literally) through a glass, darkly.

The Hon. David, who had for father a belted Earl and for uncle a Duke, no less (his mother was a Fillette-Smythe, from Bangor), laughed the polite laugh of the beautifully bred, raising his cup to his lips as his eyes lightly touched upon the spectators. At a short distance from the pavilion fence he saw a man who caused him to choke on his tea. A smallish man sporting a flat cap and a black eye, looking in his direction with the fixity of one who wishes to attract the looked-at's attention.

'Down the wrong way, eh?' the Colonel said. 'Shouldn't drink the damn stuff at all, really. Chock full of tannin.'

The young man controlled his coughing; delicately dabbed at mouth, nose and eyes with a pristine handkerchief. 'Will you excuse me, sir?' He rose, to walk casually down the steps, exchanging badinage with his white-clad team mates lounging on the benches, awaiting their turn to bat or, having batted, pretending they didn't care that they made a blob, or one, or two before calamity. Virtually all the accents matched his own. This was that kind of team. The Wellborne Wanderers (named after their founder, who died at the age of sixty-four fielding at cover-point after a breakfast of kedgeree, kippers and champagne), men from public schools' first elevens and even county players, current and recently retired; a loose connection coming together at weekends, teaming whoever was available to thrash village sides; which is all one can do, nowadays, to show the peasants their proper place. Sometimes, because cricket is quite unpredictable, a village thrashed them. As today, nearly. They were all greatly obliged to the Hon. David, who stepped in nobly, just when the bastards were getting above themselves.

The man in the cloth cap began to make furtive little jerks of the head as the elegantly flannelled figure came out from the gate in the small white fence. Perhaps he was going psst—psst; but this is doubtful. The sound would have focused eyes. It was very quiet here, the people concentrated upon cricket. The Hon. David made his way, a smile here, a nod there, a murmur here and there, to a small and sometimes (but not on this day of the year, when the Nobs played their annual fixture here) breath-stopping urinal behind the pavilion. No cubicles, just a well-pissed-in gutter, corrugated iron all around. Here, having gained the gutter, he unzipped, spread his feet and let it all hang out.

Almost immediately the man in the cloth cap appeared beside him to do likewise, and he had a goodly quota. He muttered from the side of his mouth: 'Thought I'd better see you, Guv.'

'What the hell are you doing here?' the Hon. David whispered back. Soft plashing gave the obvious answer; but the obvious answer he was not seeking.

'Had to see you.'

'For Christ's sake—not here. I've told you—'

'Bertie's dead.'

'Bertie?'

'Yeah. And I fink Georgie is, too.'

Bertie? Georgie? Who were . . . ? Oh—the man's friends. Or associates, or whatever. 'What do you mean, dead?'

'He done 'em. Young Roddie.'

'Done them?'

'Belted Bertie, didden he? And then he comes at us with that fucking van. She was still in it wiv him. I nearly broke me fucking neck, had to jump into the hedge. He got Georgie. I'm lucky I wasn't blinded. Hit a fucking tree wiv me eye.' The plashing had ceased; but the man remained in classic pose, blinking now at the Hon. David. Very disturbed, whispering jerkily; and that tree certainly gave him a nasty shiner.

The Hon. David was not looking at him. This haven was erected on a timber frame. Between corrugated iron walls and corrugated iron roof was a gap. A tall man standing here could see out. He was a tall man. His eyes scanned. Nobody coming. Only the teams and those who knew it was here came to this pissoire. The ignorant and those farther away used hedges, or trees in the wood.

He said: 'Where was this?' And when he had been told: 'What were you doing there, for Christ's sake?' Panic viciousness now, in the hiss.

'We was at the races, wadden we? We see 'em there. Thought we'd bring 'em in—like you said. You said you wanted him brought in.'

'You stupid bastards.'

'We fort you'd be pleased.'

The Hon. David had no clear idea still as to what had happened. The cloth cap man was in a condition of extreme agitation. Speakers in this condition normally believe that pictures dancing indelible before their shocked eyes are equally vivid to the listener. The full pattern emerges from them bit by bit, drawn by question and answer. Here, there was no time. At any moment men could come, seeking ease. Or somebody, having seen them go in, would wonder what they were up to in there. People think the worst of men who stand a long time side by side in a lavatory; and it was important to the Hon. David that people think the best. So he said:

'We can't talk here. Be in the potting shed this evening.'

'Yus. Right.'

Both men restowed, making the leg-flex common throughout the entire social structure, and the Hon. David, zipped, stepped out again into the sunshine, strolling with all the insouciance a shaken man can muster back to the pavilion. The cloth-cap man did not appear publicly at all. He slipped into the fringing wood and away through the trees.

The sun was moving down the sky now, towards the

loveliest of cricket field time, when the whites and greens are gilded and small clouds form motionless, plum-purple and dove grey above the horizon. Quiet voices. The crisp clapping that greets good work quiet and sudden, dying on the quiet air. Here, to run the cup of peace over, one wood pigeon went kook-koo-koooo very softly, all fuzzy-edged as though his voice were wrapped in velvet, being carefully preserved for flat-out starring in tomorrow's dawn chorus.

The Hon. David walked through it all, and now he saw and heard none of it. What had happened? What in hell had happened?

In the lane with the bloodstains, in the wood near the pretty hamlet of Upton Richard, the police by now were treating what happened as murder.

CHAPTER 5

A little time elapses between when a body or bodies is/are found and the time when the police are freed officially to mount a murder hunt. This is because a policeman must not treat a body as dead, even though it be decomposing, dug up by a rabbiting dog after weeks under a sandy bank, until a doctor (normally a Home Office appointed pathologist) has pronounced it so. Minds jump the gun, of course, eyes are probing, clues being noted; but of physical effort there is none until the doctor has arrived, and knelt, and fiddled about, and spoken. On a Sunday particularly, it takes time even to reach a doctor. The buggers all seem to be out on the golf-course, and are inclined to finish the hole even after the call arrives to summon them.

Today the delay was not unduly great. One hour approximately between the report call to Percy and when the doctor, clad in Norfolk jacket and golfing plus-fours, straightened from his examination and turned to the Chief Superintendent, here already, flanked by Sergeant Rosher and young Patrolman Hopper, who came on from the lane as soon as they heard the news.

The doctor, a fussy little plump man with a bellicose eye, said: 'All right, Mr Fillimore, you can go ahead. Not much doubt about it. That one seems to have a depressed fracture of the skull. Blunt instrument, I should say. That one appears to have been crushed. Multiple fractures, extensive surface injury. You understand that this is my preliminary examination. I can't commit fully until I have them on the slab.'

Of course Percy understood. He understood well, from long familiarity, that here was a fussy, self-important little bugger boosting his considerable ego. Aggravating, when your own gut is rumbling with pre-show nerves, and you are standing beside an enemy lately given a hideful of verbal needle and now enjoying a gloat. Cause of death was obvious, even at layman's glance, and it stamped truth on to Rosher's story. Sod it. A snap trembled on his tongue, directed at the doctor, telling him not to be such a pompous twat. But a pompous twat the man was, and ever would be. So he merely said—and the snap was in it—: 'Thank you, Doctor.'

He nodded. Scenes of Crime men, Forensic Squad men, the photographer and various bods moved forward. When their necessary jobs were done, the corpses would be stuffed into canvas bags and lifted on to the waiting stretchers, to be carted out from this pretty wood and away, to the cold stone slabs and the last macabre indignity of post-mortem. Best, if you can, to die of natural causes.

Nobody can deny, it *is* a pretty wood. All that is left of a forest where kings and nobles once hunted the wild boar and peasants. You reach it now from a lane one mile on the town side of the lovely hamlet called Upton Richard, which—the lane, not the hamlet—peters out to a rutted cart track. Odd lovers use it; but in general, the only people who go there are woodsmen, who have made a little clearing bordering the track, littered with grubbed-up stumps and chopped-up logs, strips of bark and wood chips. In this clearing, unconcealed, the battered car with the bodies stood.

It had been driven five miles from where Rosher saw the battering happen. All the way through those lanes that webbed the Ordnance Survey map. The driver's side front door, badly crumpled, must have hung open through the trip, since very obviously it could not be closed. And a wonder it is that the offside front wheel turned at all, the way wing and headlamp were scrunched in against the tyre. When searching police came upon it the crushed man was lolled in the back seat, the clobbered one half lying across him. Now, both were stretched among the wood chips. Superintendent Fillimore eyed them and the scene sombrely, without appreciation of sunshine limelighting this cleared space, dappling prettily through the trees around.

He said to Sergeant Rosher: 'You understand that all leave is cancelled?'

'Uh-huh,' the sergeant went; and his impassive features (almost human, a waggish colleague said of them) carefully hid elation. He didn't care a monkey's about leave, day leave like this or annual vacation. When they came he endured them, that's all. What he did care about had reversed itself, it was coming good; and in his heart a birdie sang. As further mask he whipped out that great handkerchief. All knowledgeable personnel braced. Those not informed or working with back towards him jumped violently as he sent his ringing clarion triumphantly through the boskiness.

Reprehensible, perhaps, that a man should feel chortling elation in the presence of ugly death; but be fair. A policeman sees so much of it: by the road accident that inflicts injuries more hideous than your average murder; by stroke and seizure and all the sudden calamities that descend upon flesh which, being departed abruptly or all at once on the way, leaves behind shocked families who don't know what to do, so they call the police. A blown-up gas oven is no fun, nor is an old man done to death by fire. Gut-reaction to every such incident would turn a useful copper into a gibbering neurotic. Or into a saint, living in a cave off roast locusts (if you can still get them) and praying by night and by day, deliver us from evil. A policeman is well aware that every single moment of every single hour, right around the clock, somebody, some-where, is being abruptly converted into a corpse.

And after all, he had reason for elation. Here he was, out from under with his every action vindicated. Nobody was going to ask now what he was doing up on that hill. Not with diabolic intent, they weren't.

On the contrary, kudos might well accrue. The pen-dulum had briefly hiccupped. Now it had said pardon and was on the way again. Going up. He said uh-huh, went through his trumpet routine, and stood in singing silence between his narrow-eyed, narrow-lipped and narrow-bodied superior and a young, ingenuous-toothed American.

Percy spoke again when the bodies were on the move, being joggled right down this cart track to where the lane began; because if ambulance and cars came up here, they'd create the problem of passing each other to get out again, or of all reversing in a solid column whenever one needed to move.

'Inspector Cruse should be here soon, Sergeant. I leave you to deal with whatever is necessary until he arrives. You know where I am, if you need me.'

Need you? I need you like I need carbuncles. 'Right,'

said Sergeant Rosher, and Percy turned away. He would go now with the bodies, to watch the autopsy. The chief investigating officer usually does. Well, you never know what will show up calling for very close scrutiny; and the doctor is not there to think, only to carve with his nasty little knives and saws and things. A good autopsy carried out by a dedicated pathologist can raise wonder in the civilized mind as to whether surgical men are indeed the devoted and kindly servants of suffering mankind, or whether the sadistic bastards actually enjoy it.

So the sergeant stood at the edge of the wood as his superior walked away, and he said to the young American: 'Took a fair hammering, didn't it? Somewhere there's a van to match.'

'Uh-huh,' Gaylord said. Even a cop of not many years service, as he was, can absorb without too much upset the gruesome truth of death by violence. Already his mind had reverted, and he was more engaged with his private affairs. 'Er—reckon I'm needed here?'

Rosher's thick lips twitched with sudden amusement. Needed, lad? Whoever needed you? I got saddled with you somehow, that's all, I need you like I need Percy. The new elation gave an Old Blubbergut edge to his joviality. 'I reckon we might just manage, son, if you fell down a rabbit hole.'

Young Hopper's teeth flashed. He was acclimatizing rapidly, and he knew this for a joke. He glanced at his watch. 'Only we're invited out to dinner. It's a quarter after five now, they're picking us up at seven.'

'Nobody's going to hold you here, son.' The monkey man was grinning. What big, beige teeth he had. 'Not even on duty, are you?'

'I guess not, officially.' Nobody had told him what he was supposed to do with his Sundays.

'I should nip off, then. I'd run you back myself, but it looks as if I'm lumbered. There'll be plenty of cars going backwards and forwards—one of 'em'll give you a lift.'

'Yeah. Fine. Okay, Al. I'll see you.'

There were, as Rosher prophesied, plenty of cars coming and going between the wood and the station. One of them took him aboard and dropped him off close by his hotel. When he entered the suite he knew that he had made one error, when he left it. He had failed to hide the bottle, or take it with him, or empty it down the bathroom sink. The edges of her voice were fuzzy when she called from the bedroom.

'That you, Jiminy?' Sometimes she called him Jiminy Cricket, for fair enough reasons. The only possible diminution of Gaylord is Gay, and these days the word has unfortunate connotations. Or Lord, and no liberated lady will call her husband that. Facing the problem squarely, she settled for Jiminy Cricket. The only Hopper (and blame the gag on her) who made it all the way to the top.

'It's me.' He passed through the living-room, in to where she sat at the dressing-table, brushing her pretty hair. Altogether pretty, she looked, wearing her dressing-robe. That damn bottle and glass stood beside her beautification bottles and jars, very handy. Amber liquid in both.

'Hi,' she said. 'Thought you weren't going to make it.'

He adopted Rosher's phrase. 'Got lumbered. Couple of bodies in a wood.'

She did not ask whose bodies, or how it happened, or what wood. In a fair attempt at the stiff-lipped British accent she sent the phrase up. 'Got lumbered. Tewwibly, tewwibly sowwy, old boy, I'm afwaid you've got lumbered.'

He made his smile, looking from behind at her reflected face in the mirror, assessing her condition; using the same exaggerated accent, the same bantering tone for cover. 'Hev Ai? Hev Ai weally? Demn bad show.'

She read his eyes. Not difficult, they had passed this way before. 'Yeah—I'm elevated. Not loaded—it's a lie, anybody says I'm loaded. I'm just a little bit elevated. On Scotch whisky. Johnnie Walker. Walker and Hopper were two little men, they never awoke till the clock struck ten.'

'How elevated?' he asked. He had to say something, and the more she talked the better he could gauge the situation. And he had to keep it easy. Get her uptight and obstreperous, anything could happen.

'Elevated enough,' she said, 'to face with equam— equamimity a forthcoming desert of sheer fucking bore-dom.'

'They're nice people,' he said. 'They seem like nice people.'

'Sure, sure they are.' She put on again her British accent. 'How d'you do, Mrs Hopper. Naice of you to hop in.' It seemed somehow to bug her lately, the fact that her name had become Hopper. She often took these little shots at it. Like now. 'Hopper. Mrs Hopper. Now there's a name to juggle with.'

'Could have been worse.' Hanging on to the smile, keeping it easy. 'Could have been Katzenheimer.'

She took a drink. Picked up the little brush that bestows mascara. 'So what's wrong with Katzenheimer? I won't hear a word against Katzenheimer. All the Katzen-heimer's are stinking rich.' She was leaning forward, lovely face screwed as a face must screw when a small black brush is applied to the upper lashes, stroking up and out-ward. 'Damn,' she said. 'Now see what you've done, I've smudged it. Go and have your shower or something, you make me nervous.'

'Yeah,' he said. 'Sure.' And he went on into the bath-room, thinking: That's the trouble, isn't it? You're always nervous. At these times more than nervous—running scared. You don't see people any more, you make ogres,

and all the flip sneering is to cut 'em down to size. Only
they won't come down if you can't get at a bottle.

One of the chief reasons why this hotel had been
selected for their accommodation was because it had better showers than any other in town. Other places, if you
wanted a shower you fitted a spray attachment and stood
up in the bath. Here, you had bath and a separate shower
cubicle. The mayor, who had been there, said that in
their homeland Americans spent most of their spare time
under the shower built in to every house; and although he
agreed with Councillor Mullins (this was during commit-
tee discussion in chamber) that the young man didn't look
like having a lot of spare time, he understood Mrs Hopper
was coming with him, and she would. The matter was
then put to the vote, and all in favour said aye.

He came back naked, drying himself on one of the big,
clean-smelling towels provided abundantly, to encourage. As the manager often said, a clean guest is a good
guest. She, too, was out of her dressing-gown now and
standing, surveying her wonderful body in the dressing-
table mirror. Fairly steady, he noted, on her feet.

'Not bad, is it?' she said, cupping her breasts in her
hands. 'The older I get the more they'll droop. Know
that? The nipples won't always point up, you know.
They'll all sag down, like a hound dog's ears. Will you
love me when they all sag down like a hound dog's ears?'

'Better get dressed,' he said. 'They'll be here soon.' He
saw a picture once, reproduction in a book. Venus
Observed, or something, by a Spanish artist called Vales-
quez. If not Spanish, Italian. Viewed reclining from
behind, with a cupid or something. His wife had the same
exquisite back, the peach-bloom buttocks. No cupid, but
her breasts were bigger.

'You can talk,' she said. 'Look at that. Why don't we
take it back to bed?'

'No time.' But as always when he had her with him

naked, he wanted her and it was beginning to show. He crossed to the drawer where he would find — he knew he would, because he sent the laundry away himself — clean shirts and underwear. 'We're going out, remember?'

'Who wants to go out? Sex is better.' But she crossed to the bed where her evening dress lay and began to don brassiere and pants. He was tying his tie when the internal telephone buzzed. He crossed to answer.

'Yeah? Hallo?'

'Mr Hopper,' said the desk clerk. Or clark, if you were British. 'Mr and Mrs Girdon-Ramsey are here.'

'Ah. Tell 'em we're — er — about ready. Will you? We'll be right down.'

'One moment, sir.'

'*You'll* be right down,' said his wife. '*I* have to go to the can. No — you won't be right down, you have to do me up.'

'Mr and Mrs Girdon-Ramsey suggest that they wait for you in the bar, sir,' the telephone said.

'Yeah — fine. Fine. Tell 'em okay — we'll be right down.' He put the phone back in its cradle. 'They're downstairs,' he told her.

'For Christ's sake, I know that. Who did you think I thought you were talking to, God?'

It took five minutes, her going to the lavatory, washing to the elbows and climbing into her dress. Three minutes, for him to finish his dressing in a dark suit that people back home who knew England had said would be okay for evening wear, and if it wasn't he could always hire. The two-minute discrepancy he used up in watching her, and zipping her in when she needed it.

As they left the suite — it grew on you, that suite, all those buffs and browns. Kind of tasteful, if not quite to his taste — he said: 'Easy tonight, honey, huh? You know — it's kind of — well, these things are kind of important.'

'Shit on you,' she said. '*I'm* kind of important.'

The hotel's buff and beige fixation continued right into the bar; but the browns gave way to deep red in thick-piled carpet, the red repeated on the bar stool upholstery. Two small alcoves and the leather bar front were a toning red, and the chairs at the alcove tables gold-framed and red-seated. Behind the bar stood a wavy-haired man, black-bowed and white-jacketed, whose immediate thought the first time Gaylord came into the bar—repeated every time since—was: What a pretty mouth he has. On two of the bar stools, close beside the pea and cashew nuts, two people sat, one larger than the other.

The large one rose, beaming. 'Good evening, good evening,' he cried, out of a quarter-melon mouth, eyes crinkling in a great moon face, utterly bald above. He wore a tuxedo, with a neat black bow. 'Here we are, then, eh?' Better-looking teeth than most Englishmen, but they all came adrift if he chewed toffee.

'Good evening, sir,' said Gaylord, beaming whitely in response to that white beam. 'Sorry we're a bit late.'

'Not at all, not at all. Molly m'dear, this is Mr O'Hopper.'

'Heowjedo,' the small lady said, all in one word without using the lips; and she must have been small because she perched on the bar stool like an elegant fairy. An ageing fairy with the rather slanty-eyed, pointed-nosed look. Under the careful coiffure, possibly were pointed ears.

'How do you do.' Not so much at this moment, because he was a mite apprehensive concerning his wife; but normally this was a real hoot to young Hopper—the way they said heowjedo, lips frozen into the greeting smile, a nation of ventriloquists. And nobody told anybody, nobody said, well, I've got this pain in the ass and it gets worse all the time and I think I'm coming down with quinsies. No—the proper response was heowjedo. Now he said it himself; but as a tyro, not come as yet to full

mastery. He could not entirely lip the words into one.
'How do you do,' he said. 'Er—Mrs Girdon-Ramsey.
Er—may I present my wife? Angelica. We call her Angie.
Angie—Mrs Girdon—er—Ramsey. And—er—Mr Girdon-
Ramsey.'

'Heowjedo,' the little lady said again. Social beaming
had her face all wrinkled up and she was gone a bit at the
throat. The hair seemed very black, for a fairy of her age.
Even so, there was something attractive about her. A
sparkle of personality. Nice thing to have, it lasts longer
than the skin.

'Heowjedo,' said the melon-faced man. If he lacked his
wife's sparkle, he made up for it by carrying the family
weight. Bulky, he was.

Gaylord could feel the tension in his wife. You never
quite knew which way it would take her, facing new
people. Sometimes her bright beam (to him; not to
them—they said what a lovely personality she had) was a
cry of fear. Where the fear came from, who could say?
Nothing in her background spoke of traumatic child-
hood, her parents were nice enough people. When it took
her beaming she gushed, brightly garrulous like a child
trying too hard to please. But sometimes there was no
beam. She tightened into silence; and when she did speak
there was a mocking, defensive sarcasm in it.

She was not beaming now, and it bothered him. She
simply said: 'Hi.'

'Well, now,' said Mr Girdon-Ramsey, working hard at
host. 'What do you say to a little drink before we go?'

'Little drink nothing,' she said. 'Make it a big one.
Scotch.'

The smiles beatifying the Girdon-Ramseys ossified for a
very fleeting moment. The insensitive would never have
noticed. Gaylord was not insensitive. Smoothly they re-
pinned, and the man said: 'That's the ticket. What about
you, Mr O'Hopper?'

Angelica spoke again, the vocal blur showing. 'It's Hopper. Plain old Jiminy Hopper. I'm Mrs Hopper.'

'Ah,' said Mr Girdon-Ramsey.

'Thank you, sir,' Gaylord said. 'Just a small scotch.'

The bulky man turned his baldness to the bar. 'That's two scotch, Fred. One a double. And two small gins. With tonic.'

'Coming right up, sir.' The wavy-haired barman picked up glasses, wondering what you had to do to catch the butch homme's eye. Wasted, he was, on a bit like that—a born lush, if ever he saw one. And he'd suffered enough to pick them on sight, fifteen years in the licensed trade. Women! He couldn't *think* what people saw in them. And a lush woman was *terrible*. This one would be the private type—a week here, and she'd never been in before. He couldn't say he'd missed her.

There is a social custom. It devolves upon the host. He must suggest, before his guests leave a bar, that everybody have another. Some time of quite smooth chit-chat later—they were really rather good at it, this hyphen-handled team—Mr Girdon-Ramsey said: 'What do you say to the other half?'

'Pardon me?' said Hopper.

The man translated. This was not his first American, he knew the sudden glaze that comes to politely smiling eyes, the freezing of the teeth. 'Care for another?'

'Make it another big one, old boy,' said the lovely young wife, in what she obviously intended as send-up of his accent.

Not really the best way to set about procuring a happy evening.

At about the time when the Hoppers sat down to dine, and Rosher, gone home, was tearing at a flannel-flavoured supermarket chicken with variegated frozen veg in a house so silent he could hear his own brown munching, the Hon. David Lawney was standing in his potting shed, wearing a smart blazer over his cricket gear and listening to a full account of what happened to Bertie and Georgie.

He said, when the cloth-capped man finished: 'You must be bloody mad. You must all be bloody mad.' It takes a little time, for the shaken mind to transmute into the past tense entities lately living.

'We fort you'd be pleased,' the cloth-cap man said.

'Pleased? With two of you dead?'

'We didn't know we was going to be dead.'

'What the hell was Bertie doing, going after him with a shooter?'

'You know Bertie, it don't really mean nuffin. He ain't never shot nobody, has he? He's—well—you know what he's like, about John Wayne and that, he just likes to wave a shooter about, doan he? It wadden even a real one, was it? They're only what they call reproductions, ain't they? I mean, they doan fire or nuffin.' A peculiarity common to most of the small-time bent: they talk almost entirely in query form. And what is true of the past tense and brighter wits is doubly true in the dim.

'Morons!' said the Hon. David. 'You—you—morons!'

'We fort you'd be pleased,' the cloth-cap man protested. 'You said to bring him in—'

'Not with a bloody gun!'

'I told you, ditten I? It *wadden* a fucking gun.'

'He thought it was, didn't he?' Of course he did, and reacted fast. He didn't look dangerous, that boy; but he must have been. The gun—that's what did it. And what would the bugger do now?

'All right!' The cloth-cap man—his name was Albie Chater—showed deep upset. Suffering still, of course, from shock. His eyes, his voice took on belligerence. 'All right—so you tell us how we was going to bring him in. He's a bastard, that boy. There was two of 'em in there, counting her, wadden there? And he used to be a judo wallah, ditten he? So how was we supposed to get him to drive his fucking wagon along here?'

'You didn't, did you, you stupid bastards? Two of you got killed. And you left them dumped in a mangled car in a wood.'

'What was I supposed to do? I couldn't take 'em out on to the main road, could I, the bloody door wooten shut. One bleeding squad car, we might have been breathalysed.'

Given the circumstances under discussion, a strangely anti-climactical pre-occupation. But the mind, shocked, dodges about in a very peculiar way. The everyday concern of men who drink and drive is the possibility of being asked to breathe into the bag. There was a grain of sense in it, too. Initially, the stopping of a battered car with lolling passengers late on a Saturday night is made with the bag in mind.

'I suppose you'd been drinking?'

' 'Course we'd bin drinking. Won a bit, hadden we, at the races? And the beer tent's open right froo the meeting, ain't it?'

'Where is this wood?'

'I dunno, do I? I ain't a bleeding native. Christ!' The cloth-cap man flared suddenly. 'Look—Bertie had just bleatin' died, hadden he? He was breavin' when I picked him up. So I'm driving along trying to find a way out with Georgie all flopping about on the passenger seat and I'm having to hold him up, and Bertie starts fucking rattling, doan he? And then he gives this horrible groan and falls over, doan he? See if you'dda done any better.' There is no doubt about it, Albie had known a hard night. All this, and a smite in the eye from a tree. He added, aggressively: 'And I was running out of petrol, wadden I?'

The Hon. David exuded no sympathy. He snapped, in the tone of one foreborn into the control of minions:

'Keep your voice down. So now we have Bertie and George dead in a traceable car. I don't suppose you even removed the number plates.'

' 'Course I did,' said Albie indignantly. 'What do you fink I am?'

It was a beautiful vehicle, the car in which the Hoppers travelled with Mr and Mrs Girdon-Ramsey from the hotel to their home. Plenty of room for four in the back, where they all sat on luxurious upholstery, separated from the chauffeur by a glass partition. Not much conversation on the way, and when they arrived nobody moved until that chauffeur, in green jacket and breeches with a peaked cap, came impassively to open the door; when they all stepped out at the imposing entrance to a new twelve-storey block of luxury flats and purred to the penthouse in a padded elevator. Or lift. Walked through the hushed, plush, fountain-tinkling entrance hall first, of course.

The penthouse was something to see. From the small but beautiful foyer—a maid met them here, to take coats. They called her Rogers, and she actually wore a frilly cap and apron. It's wonderful, what can still be done if you have the money—the feet travelled springily over lawn-like carpet to the airy, spacious, altogether eye-boggling open-plan living-room, with its great view over the town to the country beyond, its mixture of what were, surely, priceless antiques and superb modern furniture, and a mahogany staircase with open treads and slim brass (copper?) banister going up to whatever further sybarite region reposed above.

Dinner itself, though beautifully prepared and presented and nicely served by the maid called Rogers, was not the roaring success it should have been. Blame for this should be given, if it must be given at all, to the guests. Young Hopper tried hard; but a man in his situation is torn inevitably between social duty and the wish that he could take his wife home and shove her under wraps, the last heightened by the fact that this was not a mere dinner invitation. Had he not come from the town he came from, he would not have been here at all.

In the event, he need not have worried too much. Apart from taking two apéritif gins where everybody else took one, and making good time over the wines served with dinner, she did nothing truly regrettable. In fact, she began to chat quite charmingly with the steak upon the table (the British tend to serve steak to Americans, being persuaded that they nosh upon T-bone, day in, day out); about the town back home which both Girdon-Ramseys knew, having been there, and the differences between that town and this. Perhaps she was inclined to slur and even to ramble, but she extended hands across the sea. Pity was, she had already put the mockers on.

Of the two Girdon-Ramseys, the female had the better of it. Easy enough for a woman to chat with another woman, so long as the other woman chats. It never floors a woman to come upon another woman drunk, or tupping with the vicar, or indulging in any form of depravity, because she always knew that woman fully capable. With men, it is different.

There are thousands—millions—of years of inherited chauvenism between a man and sexual justice, and it will not pass out of the blood in a generation. To a man, a young man drunk is, other things being equal, an amusing sower of wild oats in a tolerable tradition; but a pretty young woman drunk is a trollop, and if he is not in the queue to make her before she sobers up, it shakes him to the deep genes. Aye—and nor is this all. Men in general are better disposed towards their fellows than are women to other women; and when a man's wife puts him into embarrassment, another man will feel sympathy for him, and with the sympathy something of the embarrassment.

So Mr Girdon-Ramsey, bound by the laws of hospitality

to encourage the young man to contribute his chat-quota, found the wicket sticky. He was not helped much by the young man himself, who did try. He did try to keep his end up, but the abstracted mind will not leap freely, and subjects that might have fruited tended to perish in the bud. As, for an instance:

Mr Girdon-Ramsey introduced—of couse he did—the name of the man with whom he trafficked in the Hoppers' hometown. He was bound to. It was this direct link with a town of the same name that inspired the mayor of the day—his father at the time, but dead now—to press on with twinning; and so, all these years later, brought the Hoppers to dinner. So Mr Girdon-Ramsey said:

'Do you know Mr Schneider well?'

'Not personally, sir, no,' said Hopper. 'I wouldn't say I know him all that well.'

And then Angelica piped up. 'You don't know him at all, honey. You know you don't.'

Affectionate reproof in a slurred voice can be deadly. Young Hopper said: 'I mean—I know *of* him. I know his office and his store.'

'Ah,' said Mr Girdon-Ramsey; and added after a second: 'Nice fellow.'

So that one died. Not a very promising topic, agreed; but almost any topic can fly off anywhere, if everybody is heading the ball. And look where this one went. Straight into the realm of the lead balloon.

They parted as soon as they decently could. The chauffeur was gone—they have unions now, who see to it that they do—so farewells were exchanged with the lady in that pile-carpeted foyer, and Mr Girdon-Ramsey took them down in the padded elevator to drive them home. 'The Rolls goes home with Riley,' he said, 'and the Daimler's in for service. We'll borrow the boy's car. It's in the garage. Might amuse you, a ride in a Jag.'

He shepherded them from the elevator through a side

door that led to a cavernous underground garage, obviously serving the entire apartment block, where they boarded a smart and rakish Jaguar. Standing close by the wall alongside it was a tallish van, covered with an off-white canvas shroud, but Hopper took very little notice. He was fully engaged, folding his wife into the low and—but this, the manufacturers would never admit—rather cramped back seating.

When they were gone, Mrs Girdon-Ramsey let the social smile flutter from her face, turned, crossed the foyer and the elegant living-room and mounted the mahogany stairs. Up there was a landing—more a prom-enade really, all that rich carpeting and fine pictures on the walls—inset with several differently coloured doors. She opened the yellow one. To a good-looking lad reading a novel, lying on the bed within, she said:

'You can come down now, if you want to. They've gone.'

'Uh-huh,' he said, turning a page.

A woman cannot simply leave a room, when a loved one addressed in it has paid her no attention. She has to shove, to obtain confirmation that she is indeed there. 'I can't think why you had to shut yourself away up here,' said Mrs Girdon-Ramsey. 'It's hardly—well—the thing.'

The lad confirmed her existence. He looked at her. 'You didn't tell them I was here?'

'When I say I won't, I don't. You should know that. But I think it's very rude of you not to say hallo, at least.'

'He's a copper,' said the lad quite mildly. 'I just don't enjoy eating with cops.'

'Don't be silly,' his mother said. 'He's not a real police-man, he's an American. A very nice boy. Wish I could say the same for his wife.'

The Jag travelled swiftly through streets not traffic-jammed at this pleasant evening hour, and set them down

on the pavement outside the hotel. Hopper, his wife
beside him, bent over to speak through the open window.
'Drink before you go, sir? Bar's open. Or we can have a
little something sent up.'

'Thank you,' said the man behind the wheel. 'Think I'd
better not. Drink and drive, you know. Work to do in the
morning.'

'Ah. Well—thank you for a very pleasant evening.
Enjoyed it very much. Haven't we, dear?'

By now her words slid downhill into each other; but she
replied enthusiastically, agush with social charm. 'Wunnerful. Wunnerful evening. Very. Can't remember when
I enjoyed a nevening so much.'

'Our pleasure,' said Mr Girdon-Ramsey. 'Well—good
night, Mrs Hopper—Mr Hopper. We'll have to arrange
another get-together.' He smiled widely, let in the clutch
and drove away, without saying when.

The beam left young Hopper's face now. When a man
has the offending woman alone, his eyeballs harden with
righteous wrath. Stiff-faced, he snapped: 'Okay, so you
fouled me up. Happy?'

'Who fouled who?' she demanded. People drunk are
invariably quick to take umbrage. She was, and he knew
it; but he was too angry to care. He snapped again.

'Come on—bed, before you fall down.'

'Bed, hell,' she said. 'I want another drink.' And she
turned towards where a second entrance to the hotel bar
fronted the street. Non-residents sipped here elbow to
elbow with *bona fide* residents, passing in and out
through this gilded door.

'Oh no you don't.' He shot a hand out to grip her arm.
'You've had enough.'

'Don't tell *me* what I've had' She dug painted nails in,
to break his hand away.

He did not let go. He added the other hand, gripping
both slim arms above the elbows. Shook her. 'You've had

enough—you're going to bed.'

'Let go of me, you bully,' she cried, struggling to free herself. 'Get your dirty hands off me.'

Never a situation so bad that Fate is not working to make it worse. But for a fly in the eye of PC Gordon Kenton (and a very small fly at that) the police car which he drove, with PC Wally Wargrave as passenger, would have passed this spot and vanished three minutes ago. Delayed, it happened along right now. 'Aye aye, mate,' said PC Wargrave. 'Pull in.'

He was out of the car almost before it stopped, as good policemen usually are upon such sightings. As he approached the two struggling figures, the male one said: 'You're coming to bed. Now. Do you hear me?'

'All right, all right, that'll do,' said PC Wargrave; and as the two heads turned to him: 'Is this man annoying you, Miss?'

She did the unforgivable. Not uncommon, wives in a fight often do it. 'What the hell do *you* think?' she cried, beginning to struggle again. 'Sure as hell he's annoying me.'

Hopper still kept his grip on her arms. 'It's all right, Officer—she's my wife.'

Men say that, too, oftimes, when they are caught trying to force a woman.

By now, Wally Wargrave had fastened on the accent, and the turning of heads had identified the man. It was the visiting Yank, bechrist, and here was embarrassment.

Wife? Had he got a wife? The constable couldn't remember what the local rag said. Human, in a strange town, for a man footloose to go out and pick up a woman, buy her a few drinks and how's yer father. But when he starts grappling her, half pissed on the sidewalk, and when he tries to rid himself of trouble and you by claiming her as his lawful wedded—well, he ought to be booked, really. Bloody embarrassing, though. Possibly dangerous.

This bloke was the current social pet, he was sponsored by the bloody council. 'I'm afraid, sir—' the constable began.

The bird cut in, high and loud. 'Arrest him! Go on—arrest him!' She giggled, stopped struggling as the situation registered. 'That'd be a hoot, wouldn't it? Go on—arrest him.' And she collapsed. Just like that. Passed out cold. The visiting Yank held her sagging in his arms, and he looked at two British policemen. PC Kenton had arrived by now.

'Mr O'Hopper, isn't it?' said PC Wally Wargrave.

'Hopper. Yeah. That's right.' I wish it wasn't, but it is.

'We met. Down at the station.'

'Oh. Yeah. How are you?'

'Fine. You? Er—the young lady—'

'She's my wife. She's—er—we've been out to dinner. Mr and Mrs Girdon-Ramsey.'

'Ah.' Don't want to know this one, do we, Gordon boy? Not with the name of Girdon-Ramsey attached. 'I think we'd better—er—get her inside. Don't you?'

'Yeah. Yeah—sure. I was just going to . . . er . . .' The white teeth were gum-bare in the night. Keeping them flashing, the young man swung the slim body up without even stooping. It rested in his arms, long legs dangling from the knees, head lolled back. Cor, the Britons thought simultaneously, look at the tits on this one. The Yank said: 'Yeah. I'll . . . Sure. Good night.'

'Good night, Mr O'Hopper.' Rank of patrolman doesn't merit sir. And his first name's Gayboy, or something, can't call him that. Not without knowing him very well, and even then tongue would stumble. But he's kind of a VIP, so you can't call him mate, chum, cock or china. Mr O'Hopper, therefore, let it be.

The American made for the hotel entrance, and a humiliating trek through foyer and reception hall to the elevator, a young and very nubile body sagged in his

82

arms. The two policemen went back to their garishly painted car.

Said Constable Wargrave to Constable Kenton, when they were seated inside: 'Wife?'

'He's got one over here,' Constable Kenton replied. 'Said so in the *Courier*.'

'Got a pair of Bristols on her,' said Constable Wargrave. 'Pissed as a dromedary. And he looked half seas over.'

Which proves how wise the little pig was when he got up and slowly walked away. Close to the bucket, the tar slops over.

CHAPTER 6

Many different lines of enquiry are pulled into action simultaneously at the discovery of murder, or very violent death pointing to it. Which particular direction these lines will take depends upon the circumstances surrounding the deed; but they will certainly tie in the Forensic Squad, the Scenes of Crime men, photographers, specialists in subjects you would never believe, a great deal of arduous brain-bashing by high brass, and an awesome amount of sheer foot-slogging graft by CID rankers in plain clothes, many of them looking more like policemen than they did in their uniform days. Particularly about the feet, after weeks of it.

When two dead men are found in a battered car, and bloodstains in a lane, the initial questions are obvious. Who are they? Do their groups match up to the blood? Who killed them? And why. Corollary to the last two: who owns the car? Who battered it? And why.

Well, it didn't take long to find out who were the two men. Albert Henry Green, 31, and George Frederick

Harris, 32 and called Wall-eye. Both known to the police, records of small larceny and rather larger assault of one kind or another. Dwellers in the frowsier areas of the big city. Race tickets found on them, and money, probably winnings; such wins confirmed in quick time by those footslogging men, contacting bookies and checking tote records. One of deceased favoured bookies, the other the tote.

Tracking the car was not so easy. The number plates were missing. Engine and chassis numbers had been skilfully erased, suggesting that one, two, three—any number of vehicles had been cannibalized to do it a power of good. That engine came from a more malignant, much faster car than the one fitted on a family saloon production line, when such things are working.

So on the Monday morning, the new Chief Constable sat in his office debating the matter with several grave men, including Detective Chief Superintendent (Percy) Fillimore and Detective-Inspector (Young Alec) Cruse.

He said: 'Car thieves, one presumes?'

'It would appear so, sir,' said Chief Superintendent Fillimore. 'City are checking all the known gangs there. We have only Herbert Johns, and I doubt if it's one of his. We're seeing him, of course, but they're city men. Not known as car merchants, but the record says they're bent enough for anything with money in it.' Car stealing is so simple, it is not easy to say who has dabbled and who has not. Whip a car, run it in to a garage with which you have no connection, collect and depart. Tempting, a few hundred quid for half an hour's work, only outlay a piece of bent wire. And you can pick that up in the street.

'What about the driver?' There had to be a driver. Stiffs don't drive themselves, nor do they remove numberplates.

'Name's Albie Chater, sir.'

'Albie?'

'Albert James Chater. They call him Albie. We're going by the fingerprints, of course, they were all over the place. Some of Chater's had blood on them. No attempt made to remove. City have supplied his record, not known as a car thief but they're checking it.'

'I have it all here.' There were papers in the Chief's hands, and more on his desk. Early reports, including post-mortem findings, copies of the City Force records, Scenes of Crime measurements and the Forensic Department's buff form stating that the blood groups matched, Albert Henry Green with patches found in the lay-by, George Frederick Harris to larger patches in the lane around the bend and spatterings on the car's battered door.

The Chief studied for a moment before he said: 'I take it there's no sign of him?'

'Vanished, sir. I've got an EMTAD out.' EMTAD: Emergency Message To All Districts. Spread by radio and blower when a seriously wanted man scarpers or for any other worthwhile reason. Sooner or later, it usually produces results.

'Uh-huh.' The Chief studied a little more. 'And what about this motor caravan that Sergeant Rosher saw?'

'We're checking every van in town, sir. Or will be, as soon as Swansea sorts the registrations out. Of course, it doesn't have to be from here—might have come from anywhere. City, probably.'

'Gang feud?'

'Could be.' Hope it's not our trouble breaking out again, thought Percy. We've had enough of that.

The Chief was thinking much the same thing. That trouble happened before he came, but he knew all about it. Mad Frankie Daly died, helped to it by Sergeant Rosher. It left half the organized crime in the area headless, wide open for grabs. Nasty men came quite a long way, to grab. It made unpleasantness. Chief Constables, especially new ones, mislike more than normal unpleasantness upon the manor.

'Hmm. Where's Sergeant Rosher now?'

'In court. He has a couple of arrests.'

'Good. Good.' The Chief was a man who liked to encourage, and a copper with two arrests is at least trying. No matter that he is not here, encouraging noises confirm the philosophy. Seek 'em out and arrest 'em. 'I suggest you put him on to that. He's the only one who saw it, presumably he knows what it looks like.'

Superintendent Fillimore and Inspector Cruse received the same thought. Probably the silent men awaiting their turn to be consulted did so, too. It didn't need Rosher, who happened to have seen the van—and couldn't sort out colour details or any other specific, against the setting sun—to identify it. It needed a lot of plodding policemen, knocking on doors and asking to see the registered van belonging here, until one came up all battered down the side, and probably with bloodstains. Well, high brass is entitled to foibles, and one of the Chief Constable's was that he seemed actually to like Rosher. Cruse's thought branched independently: Know what he's really doing, don't you? He's giving Percy a directive. He knows Percy'll have the old sod stuck firm behind a desk all through the case, if he can. And the Old Man's right—too solid in the field, our dear friend and comrade, to be wasted by personal animosity.

'Right, sir,' said Percy, with a touch of stiffness. 'I'll put him on as soon as he's free. There is, of course, the matter of the damaged vehicle—the CID car.'

'Triviality, Superintendent,' the Old Man said. 'We mustn't waste valuable men on trivialities, must we?'

Bang, said Cruse's mind. Straight up the arse. And now the talk spread between all present, theory and assessment of the situation in general, Rosher slotted into place and Percy's gut rumbling.

Mr Girdon-Ramsey, JP, sitting on the magistrates' bench this fine Monday morning, showed no surprise when Detective-Sergeant Rosher, appearing for the police, stated that this august body had no objection to bail in the case of Henry Edward Croker, charged with receiving. A long-time magistrate needs no deaf aid to tune him in to wheels within wheels. Mr Girdon-Ramsey asked no awkward questions. He simply granted bail on very reasonable sureties, looking over the tops of the half-moon spectacles he wore in court, and only in court, as badge of exalted rank.

And so Detective-Sergeant Rosher came out from the lovely, mellow-brick building where justice and injustice have been meted out about equally, without fear or—except in cases concerning friends—favour, through two hundred years of the town's history. He paused on the top one of the half-dozen steps that lead up to the handsome doorway. On his left-hand side, Patrolman Gaylord Hopper. On his right, Mr Croker.

The sergeant sniffed bare-headed at the bright morning, dragging it in through hairy nostrils. He said: 'Lovely day. Could be hot later, if it doesn't turn to rain. Well, that's my part of the bargain kept, Henry. See you keep yours.'

'One cannot absolutely guarantee results, Mr Rosher,' said Mr Croker. 'You know that.'

'I'm not asking for guarantees. I'm just telling you to bloody well produce them. Right?'

'One will do one's best, naturally,' Mr Croker said. 'Good morning.' He placed his hat upon his head and walked away down the steps.

Sergeant Rosher now covered his own head, short back and sides, half-crown tonsure and all. Upon it he placed his black hat, settling it low over the brows. 'Come along then, my son,' he said. 'Back to the factory.' And he led the lad who seemed, somehow, to have become firmly tied to him down the steps in the wake of Mr Croker. With the part of his mind not caught up with his wife, the patrolman thought as they crossed to the car: How quiet their courts are, compared with ours. Nobody shouting, nobody bearing down, no loud objections. Kind of de-humanized, all polite in English voices. But they work it just the same way—this old buzzard's got an arrangement with that old buzzard, and the guy on the bench knows it. Had to be *that* guy, didn't it? Embarrassment this morn-ing I really need.

Mr Croker, when he had trundled down the courthouse steps, did not go directly home. No transport to take him; he arrived on Saturday night in a police car. He turned right and walked along to the Post Office; from where he telephoned his wife, bidding her come to collect him. Even when she had, they broke the journey to his house at a call-box in the village of Hutton Fellows, set in the open on the edge of the duck-ponded green. A careful man likes to be able to see, as he makes his private calls, what beady eye is upon him. Likewise, he uses a public booth. Private phones can be tapped.

He rang the Hon. David Lawney at the beautiful Georgian house from which generations of squires, when they could be sobered in time by faithful retainers, rolled in coach or cabriolet down to their private pew in the old, old church, to give thanks to the Lord who gave them dominion over these fair acres of fine growing land, thatched cottages and the forelock-tugging peasantry breeding like rabbits within. Also, some good hunting, shooting and fishing. Squire and peasantry both are gone now, and the Hon. David acquired the house, not by birth but by money. Of which he had very little; but even the younger sons of belted Earls must maintain certain standards, though they go a little bent to do it.

The Hon. David answered the phone and said: 'Thank God. I've been trying to get you.'

'So my wife tells me.' Severe snap in Mr Croker's normally urbane voice, and the chubby face set harder than usual. 'How many times must I tell you not to ring the house?'

'Emergency,' said the Hon. David. 'It's an emergency. Where the hell were you?'

'Your blasted tractor—it never turned up. The police arrived. I had the load of gear in the barn. I'm out on bail.'

'Oh Christ. They haven't got wind of the big job?'

'Control yourself!' When Mr Croker had to, he could bark in the tone of command.

'Did you see it on the news?'

'See what?' Don't bother to point out to the oaf that television is not fitted into police cells.

'About the two silly bastards dead. That's why Chater didn't arrive with the tractor.'

Alarm is contagious. It was nibbling at the fringes of Mr Croker's mind. 'What are you talking about?'

'It was on the news. Green and Harris. They're dead. Chater was the only one to get away.'

Shock, all over the chubby face. He only rang to rollick this aristocratic hobbledehoy for ringing him at home. Not for his ear, worry concerning complication arising from being on bail. Complication that could have spelled utter disaster, so far as the big job was concerned, had Rosher not offered a deal. He might have gone to the city nick, remanded in custody for trial by the circuit judge next time he happened this way. 'Dead? How?'

'Girdon-Ramsey—he did it.'

'Girdon-Ramsey?' More shock.

'The son. Chater's had to go underground—he came to see me. Afterwards. I've got him in the cellar.'

Mr Croker never used filthy language, and very, very rarely took the Lord's name in vain. He did it now, though. 'Jesus Christ!' he said. And at that moment the phone went pip-pip-pip. They always do, when you get to the most interesting point of any conversation. He had time—just—to shout 'Stay there!' before the thing went blup and purred in his ear like a cat with no roof to its mouth.

He fumed, redialling the number. Green, Harris and Chater were small cogs within his planning. The first two were merely strong-arm, they could be replaced. Chater—more difficult, he had a small but vital part to play in the big job. But the boy—the boy was big part, and irreplaceable.

What the hell possessed him, knocking off people? *Any* people, at a time like this, let alone people concerned in great big business with him?

Although, of course, he didn't know that. Croker himself had seen to this. The less people knew about who was concerned beside themselves, the better. He long ago learned to keep all components separate, until they came together briefly as a whole.

That Girdon-Ramsey was of the natural, and probably vicious, bent was obvious, even to Mr Croker, who until recently had no dealings with him; but rubbing people out? Now? Why? The phone rang at the far end and was answered immediately. Mr Croker fumbled another five-penny piece into the slot.

'Why?' he demanded. 'Why would the Girdon-Ramsey boy kill Green and Harris?'

'Green went after him with a gun. He smashed his skull in.'

'With a gun? Where?'

'In his motor-caravan. It wasn't a real gun, it was a toy. Then he squashed Harris. Against the car door.'

'Is *everybody* mad? Squashed Harris?'

'Ran him over. Drove straight at him.'

'Take this number down. Ring me back. Immediately.' Mr Croker dictated the booth number. That was his last fivepenny. He hung up. In only the time it takes to poke a forefinger into a few little holes, the phone rang. Without a single reflection upon the miracle of modern electronics, he clapped it to his ear. As he did so, matters came together in his brain, bludgeoned until now by shock.

This was what Rosher saw, from the top of the hill. The damaged motor-caravan, the driver, the happening—all the things he had promised information upon in return for bail and a good word at the assizes, so that he would be free immediately to oversee the big job and scarper, long before any trial—they were here. This is what the bastard saw.

Oh Christ—if they picked up the boy, who would fly the big tickle out? Small fry you can replace; but you can't just advertise in the wanted columns for a bent pilot.

'Now then,' he said. 'Let me get this straight. Green and Harris are dead. Killed by young Girdon-Ramsey. Chater's wanted, and you've got him in the cellar. For some reason, Green went after the boy with a gun. Why?'

'It wasn't a real gun. He was trying to bring him in.'

'In where?'

'I wanted to see him.'

It all got madder and madder. 'Why?'

'He's been rogering my wife.'

'So you sent them after him with a gun?' Oh, you fool, you bloody fool. It's four months now since she left you. And there are matters afoot of far greater import than who rogers your wife.

'I didn't send them at all. Not today. I just let them know that if anybody met him, I'd hand out a little something if they brought him in.'

'A little something?'

'Money.'

'What for?'

Sudden dignity in the voice of the Hon. David. 'I was a boxing blue, you know.'

And the boy, I hear, is a karate chopper, a mean and dirty fighter. He'd have minced you, with your classic little straight left, one, two, one two. You idiot, you fool—I wish he had. I wish you'd had him there, and he'd torn you limb from limb.

The cultured voice was speaking on. 'Meant to teach him a lesson. They happened to see him at the races. She was with him. Couldn't even wait to get home—she let him rut her like a sow in a back alley.' Gritted rage in it. The stupid clod.

'How do you know?'

'They could see the van rocking. Then it went very quiet. One sleeps afterwards, doesn't one?'

Mr Croker declined to comment. Personally, he liked to smoke a cigar.

The Hon. David was saying: 'That's why they tried to take him then. While he was asleep. Or near it.'

Men like the boy are never asleep. Not completely. Christ—what a mess. And it got worse.

For instance: 'What about your wife?' She was a witness, she'd been there all through.

'I don't know—I haven't spoken to her.'

'Don't.'

'I don't intend to. Not now. Do you take me for an idiot?'

Oh yes. Yes, I do. But at least you have the sense to see that nothing, except Chater's mouth, connects all this with you; and through you, me. And the big job.

But she knows who the boy is. And she knows the van. If it's been on television and radio news—and no doubt in the papers—she'll be going to the police. If she hasn't gone.

No. No—she hasn't gone. If she had, news of the boy's arrest would have been featured on broadcasts—and you would have heard it. No doubt you are listening to every one. So for reasons of her own, she hasn't been to the police.

What a mess. What a stupid mess. That's what you get for working with amateurs and stupid people. But you have no choice. You can't function without low-grade minions; and the low-grade minion, bent or legit, is inevitably stupid. Better get off this phone. Safe enough, the public telephone; but too much has been said already.

'Listen,' said Mr Croker. 'I'm ringing off. Don't phone me. If you need to make contact—if you *need*, I say— revert to the normal channel.' A note, delivered across fields. Delivered by farmhand to the barn, or tucked into a niche in a haystack, built conveniently on the Hon. David's land, close to the end of the rosy garden.

'You must think I'm a complete fool,' the Hon. David said, with what sounded like overwrought indignation.

Mr Croker said no more. He hung up and walked back to the car, and to the wife waiting patiently. As he settled behind the wheel, he asked: 'Did Lawney say anything when he rang? Did he say what it was about?'

'No, dear. He just asked for you, and when I said you weren't home he rang off.'

'Uh-huh.' Mr Croker drove the car away. Something would have to be done about the girl. And quickly. Once an enquiry started, who could say where it would lead? And he wouldn't—possibly couldn't—call off the big job so late in the day. Yes—something would have to be done about her. And quickly—if it wasn't already too late.

But what? The hard men in London would say eliminate her. Apprised, they might even see to it. Even he could recognize that it might be the safest way. But the Hon. David was an amateur, and who can prophesy how an amateur will react? And the fool still had warm trousers for her. Look what he'd done already.

The good car purred on smoothly through all that delightful country. Behind the wheel, Mr Croker; locked in thought, seeing not a bit of it.

And what about Chater? In the cellar? Should be safe enough—provided, once again, that nobody pointed the finger at the Hon. David, his house or his associates. And Chater was necessary to the job, in that he was local, and knew every street in the town.

A pretty kettle. A pretty kettle indeed. And Rosher would be right on his back. A hard man, that one. Hard as when he was Old Blubbergut, before they bust him down. Time had not softened him, nor degradation. You couldn't trust him an inch. No feed-in of information, he wasn't above trumping something up that would land him, Mr Croker, back inside within the week. Fatal, at this moment in time. The hierarchy in London, Paris, New York—they wouldn't like it a bit.

CHAPTER 7

When Patrolman Hopper, towed still by Sergeant Rosher, entered the police station, embarrassment was brought to him almost immediately. They arrived from the court just as a flock of people came, mostly scruffy, down the stairs that led to the offices of upper brass and a snugly panelled room with an uninterrupted view of the parking lot, wherein the Chief Constable presided over all. Even Hopper, unused to the appearance of the British Press-person, knew these to be reporters.

The Chief had been holding one of his personal conferences, saying—very clever at the art—as little as possible as courteously as possible. Certainly he had not mentioned Sergeant Rosher's bird's-eye view, because they all hurried by, with only a nod from those who knew him instead of a general mobbing. The sergeant led on, with jungle gait.

In the clacking passage they met Constable Wally Wargrave, he who came to the assistance last night of an assaulted lady. Late turn yesterday, day shift today. Earlies next week, nights the week after. Round and round the little ball goes. The constable came from the general duty room, and he grinned when he saw young Hopper, saying: ' 'Morning. Lovely day.'

Hopper's fine teeth flashed in reply. Almost a nervous grimace, that beam. ' 'Morning,' he said. 'Sure is.' As it was, with the cool pearly quality of diffused light that makes it seem to the recent incomer that in England day never quite comes fully.

'How's the young lady?'

'Fine. Thanks—she's fine.' He left her awake, sick and wan; but calmer. She was through it, please God. The attack was, if experience was a thing to go by, over. She would be all right now—for a time. Perhaps until the visit was finished and they were back home. What happened after, in all the years to come, was matter for future worry.

'That's the ticket,' said Constable Wargrave. 'Nothing like letting your hair down in your free time.' He winked horrendously and passed on grinning, out to where Constable Kenton waited, sitting in the patrol car that would encase them for the rest of the day.

'What was that about?' asked Rosher with no particular interest as they clacked to the CID room. He arrived and left for court this morning before Wally Wargrave and his oppo came on duty, and so did not know of the merry story going the rounds. Raising chortles, because a police station, owing to the peculiarly isolated social position of the police, is virtually a self-centred village; and villagers do love gossip. The exotic visitor, especially when circumstances blow him up almost to VIP status, is particularly vulnerable. A touch of scandal whittles him down very enjoyably.

Hopper, in the act of enclosing his teeth, stripped them again. 'Nothing in particular. Just we had dinner last night with Mr and Mrs Girdon-Ramsey. He saw us coming home.' His mind said: You'll know, soon enough.

No fool, this Hopper. The social isolation of policemen is common the world over. Already, he had spotted that only surface matters of uniform and custom, accent and cover veneer, separated these fellers from those at home. He knew how *they'd* relish the visiting Englishman, wrestling with a loaded woman on the sidewalk at night.

They came into the CID room. Young Detective-Inspector Cruse was just leaving, papers in his hand. He said: ' 'Morning.' This to Rosher. And to Hopper: 'Good morning, Mr O'Hopper.'

Was there a sort of covert reassessment in the bonny blue eye? For sure, there was a new gleam in some of the eyes that glanced up briefly before heads went down again over desks where men sat on inadequate chairs, writing in longhand or typing with one finger little bits of this and that. 'Good morning,' said Hopper.

Alec Cruse turned his six foot and muscular attention back to Sergeant Rosher. 'Seen Percy?' he asked.

'Been in court,' Rosher told him. Answer and reason all in one.

'Oh yes. Well—the caravan. You're assigned to the job. Lists of local registrations are in. Okay?' He smiled upon Hopper. Atractive smile he had. Some thought him attractive altogether, but he couldn't see it, himself. Not that it bothered him. 'If you're happy with Sergeant Rosher, Mr O'Hopper, perhaps you'd like to go along. Couldn't have a better mentor.'

'Grrmph,' went Rosher. Not pleased, not displeased. The commendation meant nothing. No offensive flattery in it, just a social thing said.

'Sure.' The white teeth were at it again. 'Surely. Okay.'
'Good,' said Inspector Cruse. 'Have a nice day.' And he went.

'Right, lad.' Rosher spoke. 'Let's get weaving.' He turned and led the way out of the room again. Hadn't even taken his hat off. Did one of the desk men speak *sotto voce*, and gather a surreptitious titter as the door closed?

They gathered up the necessary list and Rosher told Sergeant Barney Dancey, that man who entered all kinds of things in all sorts of book, that he was taking a car. When they were in it and driving away, he said: 'Doubt if it'll be local. Could have come from anywhere. The stiffs were from the city. More than likely a gang punch-up.'

'Back home,' said Hopper, 'they tend to shoot each other.'

'You'd be surprised,' the sergeant told him, 'what they get up to over here.' He smiled brownly, as one who would say: You don't have all the bastards in your back alley, my high cockalorum.

The Hon. David Lawney's wife, Veronica. Very pretty girl. Beautiful, most competent critics said. Middle height, slender built, natural (or minimally aided) blonde with fine, near-violet eyes. Married to him three years, left him four months ago. Lived now in a flat in the town, on money her father willed her. Had a man or two since, as and when she fancied. Worked before marriage as model, actress (briefly), dental receptionist and centre spread in *Playboy*. All this, and still only twenty-two. And she a vicar's daughter, named for a saint.

She met the boy Girdon-Ramsey in the Blue Dahlia Club. The town's one class night-spot, all maroon leather, gold trimmings, soft lights and intimate snuggling booths. Pretty good band, too, middle-of-the-road and rock. One of the men she'd had was the leader; and he, using the technique proven over centuries by herberts of his ilk, as part of his campaign to inveigle her to bed, persuaded her that she could well make the grade as a singer. It is every girl's wishful dream.

So this is what she was doing when she took the goaty eye of Roderick Andrew Henshawe Girdon-Ramsey, only son of a man of much lucrative business, a respected JP: singing with the band. And not doing it badly, quite unpaid. Looked gorgeous—packed far better evening wear when she left the Hon. David than your average girl singer can afford, even allowing for sugar-daddies and straight whoring. Like the man said, if all the girl vocalists in the business were laid side by side, no musician would be a bit surprised.

She kept him dangling—No, no, a man lusting does not dangle. She kept him hot for some weeks, by which time the bandleader and her vocal career both were gone into the mist. Truth was, she didn't fancy the boy all that much; and since she had no particular need for money (a shrewd vicar has plenty of time to study the stock market) or any of the other side benefits of sex, she had to fancy before she bit. But whatever may have been said of the Girdon-Ramseys, and plenty was, they bred a sticker. In the end she said all right—the races on Saturday.

There was, be it agreed, a rakish sort of attraction about him. When he collected her, not in the Jaguar but in the motor-caravan she had not known he possessed, it sparked amusement. A motor-caravan is a travelling bed. Well—she could use it or not, later, according to how the day went. His intentions were obvious.

The day went nicely. He could be a very amusing young man, a charming one when after his oats; and no woman ever born is bored or displeased, knowing herself desired and so reassured of her desirability. He splashed money about—the full fresh salmon and champagne lunch with the strawberries, big bets on the tote and so on; and altogether she enjoyed everything right up to the orgasm; until he suddenly twisted off her, produced a bonk like a stricken pumpkin—with a bloody great wrench, she knew now—and a grunt, and something like a sack falling; and squirmed naked into the driving seat and took off; slamming right through a man and a car door, as she saw for herself, being crouched with a bloodied nose by then, goggling through the windscreen and screaming.

He drove naked right out of the lane, on to the main road. Plenty of traffic here, too; one might have thought it would be noticed that he had nothing on. But of course, the cab of a motor-caravan is set higher than the seating position of your normal car, so a passing driver or idle passenger, looking, would see only the top half of his body, and she, naked also but behind closed curtains, not at all. Lots of young men strip to the waist in fine weather. Even young women tend to now, and it's lovely.

He stopped in a lay-by and they dressed. 'What's going on?' she demanded. 'What the hell's going on?' To which he replied: 'Shut your fucking mouth.' Dressed, they drove on.

He turned her off on the outskirts of town, and in her mind already was the intention of going straight to the police; but he said:

'Listen—ever seen a face done over with acid? One peep out of you—to *anybody*—I burn you all up. Get it? I'll blind you—it'll burn your eyes out. You'll be blind, and you'll be disfigured for life. Understand? And listen—it can be done again and again. You'll never know when it's going to happen again, all the rest of your life. Now sod off.'

She got out of the van, and her eyes saw that it was badly scagged as he drove away; but her mind was shocked beyond registering anything except horror. He'd do it. Or have it done, if he was unable to operate in person. She saw him drive straight through that man. He was a killer.

Oh Christ—what had she got herself into?

She went home to her small flat; and there she stayed, too shaken to go out. The television, when the news broke, told of a battered car found in a wood—she knew the wood, she had ridden through it often before she left the horse and the Hon. David—with two bodies aboard; and still she stayed inside, the door locked.

But she ran out of food, and hunger rages at last. On Monday, at lunch-time, she thought: I'll go to the café on the corner. And do a bit of shopping. And come straight back.

Still no firm intention, you see, still no plan. Shock like that goes deep, and to a beautiful girl, a faceful of acid is a terrifying prospect. Hell—it is to anybody gifted with more imagination than a turnip.

She set off now, carrying her little straw shopping-basket with the big cloth roses on it; and a car parked unobtrusively in the side street opposite slid out, passed her and stopped a few yards ahead. A man came from it, a big man in a suit, with a broken nose.

He said when she came up: 'Excuse me, Miss—do you mind getting in the car?'

'What—what—?' she said.

He reached out a fur-backed hand, gripping her arm. 'Don't make a fuss, there's a good girl,' he said. 'I don't want to have to hurt you. Let's just get in nice and quiet.'

Before she finished saying: 'Who—what—?' she found herself in the back seat. The big man landed heavily beside her. 'Right, Charlie,' he said. The car drew away.

Now she babbled. 'Who are you? I don't want . . . Where are you taking me?'

'Just for a little ride, darling.' The big man had a gruff and husky voice. The driver was a small, wizened fellow, wearing a flat hat. 'Little drive in the country. You can wave to the cheering crowds if you like, just like the queen does. Only smile when you do it. And don't holler, I don't want to have to hurt you.'

They drove out of town, through familiar country and on to a familiar private road leading off from the main highway. Through familiar gates and along the gravelled drive, stopping at last outside the lovely old house where she lived three years and last saw four months ago. The big man moved his heavy body, reaching for the door handle; saying as he got out: 'Be a good girl while I'm away. Nasty little man, Charlie is. That right, Charles?'

'Proper little bastard,' said Charlie.

The big man mounted the steps fronting the fine pediment-surmounted carved oak door. He tugged at the old-fashioned bell-pull which set up a jangle inside. Johnson came. Her husband's man. A brief word. Several, pehaps, who knows or cares? Johnson stood aside. The big man entered, and the door closed.

Johnson leading, they crossed the hall, past the three suits of armour, the antique tables set with fine crystal bowls filled with flowers, the oak settle and chest said (and rightly) to be fifteenth-century, with never a trace of worm. In the pastel-coloured room beyond, the Hon. David Lawney sat in a leather armchair, his eyes turned their way. 'Gentleman on urgent business,' said Johnson, and withdrew.

The big man approached the leather armchair. If he had an appreciative eye for antiques set in an exquisite room he did not let it show. He crossed to the Hon. David Lawney, thrust an envelope upon him, said: 'Letter for you,' turned on his heel and trod away without a glance; out from the room, across the hall and through the front door, no assistance asked of Johnson, who had unusually beetling brows for a gentleman's gentleman and stood in the hall with his arms hanging down. Gentlemen's gentle-men — a vanishing species — normally trim their eyebrows. And they study deportment. But then, nothing is what it was.

Back at the car, the man opened the back door. 'Come on, dear,' he said. 'Let's be having you.'

'I don't . . . Why have you brought me here?'

He reached in and reapplied his hairy grip, tight as a tourniquet. 'Don't let's have no argument, I don't want to break your arm. Do I, Charlie?'

'You dunno what you *are* breaking,' said Charlie from under his flat hat. 'Don't know your own strengf, you don't.'

Two, three minutes later the big man, the little man, the car, all were gone. She stood in the beautiful room facing her husband, risen now from his chair. He looked, take away the pallor and the twitchiness, very handsome. It did not make her like him any better. She exploded now.

'What the hell's going on? What the hell do you think you're doing, treating me like a—a—a—'

'Sit down,' he said. 'Shut up and sit down.' He glanced again at the letter in his hand, as if for guidance. It gave him none, except a bald directive, in brief words.

'This is yours,' it said. 'Look after it.' No signature— nothing. Not even his name and address on the envelope.

He knew who it came from, of course. Mr Croker had acted fast.

CHAPTER 8

Rosher and Hopper were out on the job. A very pleasant job, on a fine sunny morning. In common with milkmen, breadmen, paper boys, jobbing gardeners, traffic wardens, fishwives and men who pull up manholes to peer at whatever lies beneath, detectives enjoy rare days of compensation for all the times of slogging on in foul weather and fouler. This was one of them. A pleasure to be out of doors, beamed at by a benevolent sun.

The world in general does not fully realize how popular, over the past few years, the pastime of caravanning has become. Why, in truth, should it? In the starving countries in particular, they have their own problems. Sufficient, to say that the list carried by Sergeant Rosher was considerably longer than it would have been, not very long ago.

It was eleven o'clock when they set out. There were motor-caravans on the new estates that formed—still form, alas, growing wider still and wider—the suburbs of the old, most agreeable town, and some closer to the centre. They squatted in garages and on land beside cottages in the surrounding villages of Burton Richard, Doves Ambo, Patley and Wapley Bridge. These outlying fringes were scored through on his list. Other, local men would visit Mr Dodson, Mr Fogal, Mr Emmett, Mrs Britton, Mr Burppe (truly—he lived at Burton Richard). Rosher's were the inner suburbs, and the centre of town.

The American æsthetic sense responds more favourably to what is new than does the British, the eye being accustomed to relative newness from birth and the mind tuned in by a general admiration for get-up-and-build. So Hopper did not find the little semi-detached houses offensive, as sensitive Britons do. On the contrary, if the word quaint did not enter his head in its exact form, this is what he thought them, all standing neatly in neat little streets, each sprouting its own, its very own television aerial. He liked the small gardens, the roses and variegated flowers; and he shook with interior laughter at Sergeant Rosher's approach to the public. The feminine part of it, anyway—they saw women. Housewives, with the husband in whose name the van was registered gone to work. There are still women who cling to the old freedom of feet up when you feel like it and a cup of coffee, refusing to be incarcerated in factory or office by liberation.

Sergeant Rosher's technique was based on a firm belief that when charm was called for, it radiated from him. A ring at the bell or a knock upon the door; and as that door opened, revealing a woman in her comfortable housework gear, he snatched off the black hat, bared ingratiating teeth and said with enormous unction:

'Good morning, madam. Mrs Howsyerfather? We are from the police.'

'Police?' the woman would say. Quite startled, some of them looked. A Mrs Fern asked if it was about the television licence.

'Nothing to worry about.' Brown-beaming reassurance. 'Is Mr Howsyerfather at home?'

'I'm afraid he's at work.' Almost a standard answer. Not one said she was glad, glad, *glad* he was at work, out from under her feet while she pottered to a background of radio pop music, secure in the knowledge that the weekly pay packet would maintain her in her neat little queendom, three bedrooms, fitted kitchen, chintzy curtains and a back boiler for constant hot water. Plus, of course, lounge and the usual offices. Not one said it was a bloody nuisance that he ever came home. 'I'm afraid he's at work,' they said.

'Ah. Pardon us for bothering you. Detective-Sergeant Rosher.' A flash of identity card contained in a little well-matured wallet. 'I wonder whether we might just take a look at the motor-caravan registered in his name.'

She would lead them to it, in garage or garden or wherever it may be. One kept it in his greenhouse. Would you believe that? Begonias all around. None was scagged. Most were immaculate, the few wounded bearing only such minor dints as come from backing into farm field gateposts or misjudging entry into camping sites, arriving at night with a crunch and a fuck it. Back they would all go to the doorstep; where Rosher would replace the black hat, presumably so that he could snatch it off again, since this is what he did; saying:

'Thank you very much, madam. A very nice van you have there. Pity everybody doesn't maintain their vehicles so well, we'd soon have the road statistics down. Good morning.' And all this talk in a telephone voice.

On hat, and away like an amiable gorilla down the little crazy-paved or tarmac path, carefully closing the gate. And so to the car, young Hopper quaking behind him with an interior delight that took away the lingering unease engendered by Constable Wargrave and the station. Now that she was over it, he must tell Angie about the old baboon. She'd love it. She creased, when he did his impersonations.

Around twelve-thirty, several calls behind them, they sat in the car outside the gate of one of the little houses while Rosher consulted his list again. 'Next one takes us up in the world a bit,' he said. Much of his oddly-fitting joviality stayed with him between calls. Truth is, he was beginning to like having this very unargumentative, almost deferential young man with him. And it was a pleasant day, himself all easy and vindicated. 'Friends of yours. The Girdon-Ramseys.'

'Ah,' said Hopper, feeling unease flutter again. One pair of people he preferred not to see, the Girdon-Ramseys. Not yet. Not so soon after last night. Awkward enough, finding the guy was magistrate this morning. No happiness in confronting the formidable social charm of the wife right now.

There came no covert sideway flick of the eye from Rosher, looking for reaction. Still, he knew nothing about last night. Nobody had the chance to tell him, all his time at the station Hopper was with him. He folded the sheet and put it back into his pocket. 'Grub first,' he said. 'My belly's knocking on me belly-button, trying to get out.' He bared the brown teeth again to hint that a receptive smile would not come amiss.

Hopper's white beam flashed immediately. A most accommodating young man. 'Yeah. Sure. Great.'

'There's a pub. The Green Man. They do bread and cheese. Sandwiches, hot pies. Do for you?'

'Surely. Sounds great.'

Five minutes later they were seated in the beamed bar of a good old pub, and Hopper was wondering how it happened that he seemed to have paid not only for two pints of the thick-flavoured English beer, but also for his own hunk of crusty bread with butter and a wedge of strong cheese, and two hot pies, into the first of which the sergeant, having spread it liberally with mustard, was even now sinking those alarming incisors. Not that it bothered him, the bread was new and the cheese remarkable, and the pub old-worldly enough to have charm. He just didn't see how it happened, that's all.

'Cheers,' said Rosher, and raised his glass tankard briefly before swigging.

'Cheers.' Hopper, too, lifted his beer, as a man must do given the gesture, and took the obligatory swig. Once you got used to the damn stuff, it began to grow on you. Went well with bread and cheese. Bacon and egg, fish and chips. They had these combinations, and they all grew on you. He'd heard somebody mention Swan and Edgar; but although he was prepared to believe in it, it sounded unlikely.

'I don't,' said the sergeant, nodding at his beer, 'usually do this in the middle of the day.'

'Yeah—me, too,' Hopper said.

'Learned to lay off in my boxing days.'

'Were you a fighter?'

Rosher expanded. 'All-England Police Champion, three years running. Heavyweight.'

'Say—that's really something. Did a little myself, at college. Never got to be any kind of champion, though.'

'Takes dedication,' said Rosher; and went on to spend a happy half-hour—midway through which, Hopper found he had bought more beer—telling of the days when he arose, to run at dawn all over the park in the town where he was born (Bishop Adam's Park, named after a man nobody cared a damn about) clad in shorts and singlet, skipping-rope in hairy hand for use by the boating pool. He spoke of the heavy bag, and his developing thereon the hammer, smitten with which a man was smitten indeed and likely to lie down. He gave account of mighty battles won, slugging toe to toe, but not of those where the other bloke slugged harder, or first. He enjoyed himself; and to tell the truth, Hopper was far less bored than he could have been. For one thing, he followed boxing. For another: it was all grist, for Angie's hilarity later. And for yet another: he liked the old guy's voice, English and earthy now and full of strange idioms, pointing up the odd mangling when he used his public image telephone talk. Hell—he *liked* the old guy. He liked the gorillaness of him, he liked the haircut with the hole.

When food was gone and the clock showed five past one, Rosher swallowed the last of his beer and said: 'One o'clock. Better be going. I'd buy you another, but two's plenty for lunch-time. Don't want to get breathalysed, do we?' He settled the black hat, arose and led the way out of that pub, walking as ever with chest out and belly pulled in. Unfortunately, pulling in of the belly, carried too far, sticks out the bum; so that his gait—it was a salty colleague who said it—suggested that he had a banana stuck up his jacksie.

When they arrived at that block of expensive apartments, which they did without mishap, the man with depressed moustaches who presided at a desk in the fountained hall by day spoke into the blower, very respectfully, and put it down to say: 'Will you go up, gentlemen?

The penthouse suite.'

They crossed to the burnished elevator, and as they whisked soundlessly skyward young Hopper said: 'Wait till you see this place. What'd it cost over here, penthouse in a block like this?'

'God knows,' answered Rosher. 'But they should worry—they own the bloody lot.'

'All of it?'

'All of it. The whole block and a bloody sight more besides.'

'Jeez,' said young Hopper. 'Do they want to adopt a son?'

'They've already got one.'

It goes without saying that when you press the bell on that class of door, you produce a mellow chime. The maid called Rogers came and admitted them to the small but beautiful foyer, Rosher with his charm at roasting heat. Not by the flick of a lash did she hint that she remembered well dinner last night, and the young man's wife getting pissed and pisseder. All she did when she saw him was smile the restrained smile of the good servant, and murmur: 'Good afternoon, sir.' She then went to tap on a door, disappear briefly, return, and usher them through it, into that antique-strewn, eye-boggling living-room.

Mrs Girdon-Ramsey was here, sitting tiny in a great leather armchair. Without the cushions, she'd have been flat on her back. Taken any way, as individual pieces or all together, the word best fitted to the furnishing is sumptuous.

Mrs Girdon-Ramsey spoke. 'Good afternoon, Mr Hopper. We seem to be linked by destiny.'

'Seems so, ma'am.' Nothing in this eye, too, suggested that last night ever happened. The fact did not ease the young man's embarrassment. However she acted, she had a memory. She wasn't a unicellular brain.

Rosher's hat was off. He held it between hairy fists in front of his chest, and he spoke in a beaming welter of mangled vowel-sounds. 'Good afternoon, madam. Terribly sorry to burst in upon you at this hour. Detective-Sergeant Rosher. This is a—er—a colleague from America.' His style of speech, he might have said the Colonies.

'We know Mr Hopper,' said Mrs Girdon-Ramsey, either including her husband or using the royal plural. She beamed upon the boy. Enthusiastically, he beamed back.

'Ah. Of course.' Sergeant Rosher's brownstone fangs joined in the general airing.

'How can one help you, Sergeant?' asked Mrs Girdon-Ramsey.

'A motor-caravan, madam. I believe you possess one. Registered in your son's name.'

'Roddie has one, yes,' said Mrs Girdon-Ramsey. 'We haven't.'

'Ah. Of course. We were wondering if we might be permitted a glance at it. Pure routine, of course.'

'I'm afraid he's away in it at the moment. Touring Scotland. You know what boys are, never stay long in the same place.'

'Ah,' said Sergeant Rosher. 'Yes. Well—he's chosen fine weather for it. May one ask when he might be expected back?'

'We never really know. He simply goes off, and we expect him when we see him.'

'Ah. Pity.'

'Is it important?'

'No. Not at all. When did he go?'

'On Friday. Soon after breakfast.'

'Ah. Well—that more or less settles the matter. I expect you are aware that we are concerned about an incident involving a motor-caravan. But, of course, it took place on Saturday night. By which time, one imagines, your son was probably tripping the light fantastic on the bonny, bonny banks of Loch Lomond. Ha ha ha.' All smiled politely. 'Yes. Well—thank you very much indeed. Registration number SJX 127V?'

'I believe so, yes.'

'Fine. Thank you. Once again, our apologies for the intrusion.'

'Not at all.' Mrs Girdon-Ramsey smiled prettily, sitting like a fairy in her great chair. 'Is there anything more?'

'That's all, madam, thank you. We'll leave you in peace now.'

'Drink before you go?'

The sergeant spoke promptly, lying in his brownstones. 'Never while I'm on duty, thank you, madam.'

'Very commendable,' said Mrs Girdon-Ramsey; and the meeting broke up, goodwill manifest on all sides. Sergeant Rosher could not help feeling, as he followed the maid called Rogers to the door, that he had just given a practical demonstration of how good relations should be fostered between police and public. Especially when the public is wife to a JP, and might be expected to talk about it. Not that the Girdon-Ramseys were exactly common-place public, but the principle still applied.

When they were out of the way, Roddie came from his room, down that handsome staircase. He knew what had transpired, having long ago fitted a bug into the Sheraton sideboard. Useful, to know what is being said about one, particularly when one tends to return from unexplained trips coinciding with jobs that make the papers. Even the headlines, one or two of them. Not that his parents would ever connect him with them. Still, it's as well to keep tabs. He said: 'Everything jolly?'

'I cannot imagine,' his little mother said, 'why you should hide yourself away in your room like this.'

'I told you—I don't like policemen.' To her, his grin

was a sweeter thing than a five-gallon drum of Golden Syrup.

'That's no reason for getting me to lie for you. You put me in a very awkward position. After all, Daddy is a JP.'

The grin that gave song to her heart. 'You can handle Daddy.'

She laughed, delighted that they were, now as always, allies against the whole world, Daddy included, when he asked for it. 'Naughty boy. And why Scotland?'

'Just happened to think of it.' Might have been better to have said Norway. Or Spain, or somewhere. Although, if they were really on the track, they'd check ferry bookings and passport records and so on.

'Darling—' the mother's eyes were soft, tender as from his birth when they rested upon her son, her very own dimple-dumpling—'you're not in any kind of trouble, are you?' Mind you, she didn't call him that any more. He'd grown, somehow and in no time at all, to be twenty.

Oh, that irresistible grin! 'Pregnant, you mean? The tests are negative.'

'I'm not joking, dear. If you are, you must tell Mummy. I won't let you down, you know that. But I can't help if you are not *frank* with me.' Earnestly she spoke, her eyes almost moist with self-giving. 'You must be *frank* with me, darling.'

'Oh, Mother,' he said; and a vicious young bastard he was, really, but never in this world would she see it. Nor would his father, for that matter. 'For God's sake!'

'Where did you say your van is, dear?'

For a second he stiffened. Surely—surely she hadn't been down to check? She never checked on him. Never. 'I told you—I lent it to a friend.'

'You didn't say what for.'

'He needed it for a few days. Private business. That's why I have to keep it secret—I promised not to tell anybody.'

'I hope he's not up to something funny in it,' she said. 'I wouldn't want to mislead the police, if he's up to something funny.'

'What did they say, then?' Roddie asked. He knew damn well, he heard every word; but not to query could set even the besotted parent wondering how he knew, if he betrayed that he did. Not even his Mummy knew about the bug.

'They asked about the van,' said Mrs Girdon-Ramsey. 'I told them you were away in it. Just as you said I should.' On Sunday morning, he said it. If anybody comes asking for me, tell them I'm away in the van.

'Good,' he said. 'It's all right, Mummy—truly it is. Trust me.' Oo—what an invitation. Others had done that, to their cost. Had they not been so misguided, the current situation might never have happened.

'I do, my love—of course I do. Only there's a—this van. The one the police are seeking—'

He turned to her, his widened eyes showing horror rather than anger. 'Oh, Mummy—Mummy—surely you can't believe—'

Swiftly she answered him, horror matching his own in every line of her still pretty face. 'Of course not, dear. It's just that Mummy worries about you, that's all.'

There is a thing closed tighter than a clamshell, the mind of a loving mother. And now the telephone rang. It stood on a table, set close to that big picture window commanding the superb view. Mrs Girdon-Ramsey arose to answer it. Gave the number and listened for a moment. 'I'm afraid he's not here,' she said. 'He's away. I really can't say—he's touring. In his motor-caravan. No, we don't know when he'll be back. Yes. Yes, I'll ask him to ring you.' She hung up, addressing the boy. 'A Mr Croker. He wants you to ring him as soon as you get back. Urgent, he says.'

In the hall of his house near Hutton Fellows, not far away as the crow flies, Mr Croker put the telephone down and stood frowning at it. He'd dealt with the matter of the Lawney girl, unsatisfactorily but as best he could at emergency notice; but the boy presented a different and horrible problem. Mr Croker had expected—what? He didn't quite know.

That the boy would contact him? Ring him, in spite of his own strict edict forbidding calls to his home? Or get a message to him, saying something—anything—to clarify the situation? If it could be clarified.

Had he bolted? Left a great, gaping hole in the ranks through which the entire enterprise might tumble?

No—it wouldn't tumble. He couldn't let it. But if the boy was out, considerable replanning was called for; and it had to start now.

And oh—if the police picked him up, what might he say? There's no honour among thieves, only the layman thinks there is. Mr Croker was no layman. He was a pro, with a pro's knowledge of how a man will talk to ingratiate himself and save his own skin.

At last he broke his own rule. No great danger in it. Nothing much needed to be said, all he wanted was to know if the boy was there. Two or three words would be sufficient, giving the number of a public booth to be called at a given time from a similar booth. He spoke to the lad's mother; and afterwards stood frowning in thought.

Wherever the fool was, he wasn't touring in his van. Not battered as it had to be. Even if it ran smoothly, he'd need to be a lunatic to drive it on any road to anywhere, in the teeth of police and all the keen amateur detectives who listen to radio, read papers and/or watch television. Unless on Saturday night he took it somewhere, directly into hiding.

A mess. Better start planning to replace him.

But—where do you get a bent pilot? One who can legitimately participate in the town festival as a local citizen, son of a leading worthy? You don't. And without a pilot . . .

They wouldn't like this, the hierarchy. They had approved his master-plan, modified it a little and set it up from their end. A lot of work and financial investment. They wouldn't like it at all. And they were hard men. Paid well, his own cut would take care of his entire future; but they had already warned him: we don't take kindly to slip-ups.

His wife came trippety-tripping through the hall, on her way to spend a penny. 'Anything wrong, dear?' she asked. 'You look very serious.'

'Nothing, my love,' he assured her. 'Just a little business problem.'

'You work too hard, dear,' she said; and went tripping on her way. Might have stayed for more, but her penny was pressing.

When Sergeant Rosher drove Patrolman Hopper away from the splendid high-rise block, he said: 'About due for time off, aren't you? How are you working it, the same as the rest of us?'

'I don't know,' said Hopper. 'I don't think anything's fixed. One of those things, got overlooked.'

'We've only a couple more calls,' the sergeant told him. 'I'll find out when we get back to the station. You worked yesterday, didn't you? Work Sunday, you get a day in lieu of. Or overtime. But that wouldn't apply to you. Would it?'

Hopper grinned the grin. 'I doubt it—they gave me salary in advance for the weeks I'm over.'

'Take the time off, then. Spread it over a couple of half-days, trot the wife along to the pictures.' Here was the flower of benevolence, very rare in Rosher. Good day, this, and on good days there is pleasure in the right company. Hopper, undemanding and eager to please, for Rosher was the right company. He found in himself increasing liking for the boy. He heard himself repeating, and wondered that he should because sod it, in his philosophy if a man couldn't see to it that he got his fair whack, more bloody mug him: 'I'll find out about it, when we get back.'

He kept his word, too; and Hopper, by no means incapable of conducting his own affairs, let him do it; because the graceful response to a proffered courtesy is acceptance, and he was an aware young man. After the two more calls, both of which showed unmarked vans, they rode back to the station; where at Rosher's bidding they clacked along to the office that used to be his. Therein sat young Inspector Cruse, seated at Rosher's old desk, dealing in his shirtsleeves with the paperwork that is the bane, the utter bald-headed bane, of every working policeman's life. He said come in to Rosher's knuckles, and when they were inside the sergeant said:

'Doesn't seem to be anything fixed about time off for our young friend here.'

Young friend? thought Cruse in a little marvel. Bloody heck—what's happened to you? I thought you'd come to bulldoze him off your back. 'Isn't there?' he said; and addressed the Yank. 'Didn't Superintendent Fillimore sort you out?'

'Well—no,' said Hopper. 'Nothing definite. I was off last Tuesday. It doesn't bother me—I'm happy.'

'Fair do's,' the inspector said. Cheerful guy, with a grin you could get your teeth into. 'All work and no play and we'll have the coppers' union on our backs. What's on now?'

'Nothing much,' Rosher told him. 'We've been checking vans. I've got my report to make out. Few bits and pieces.'

Cruse spoke to Hopper. 'I should scarper now, if I were

you. Nothing much to interest you, unless you want to check the sergeant's spelling.' He shifted his grin to include Rosher, because you never quite knew how he'd react to a little social jest. Today, he was taking it nicely. No answering grin, but no discernible bristle.

Small problem, getting a grin out of the American. 'Wouldn't do much good,' he said. 'I can never remember how many g's in egg.'

I seem to have done it right, Cruse thought, putting these two together. They actually seem to have taken to each other. Old Blubbergut's quite easy, and the Yank seems actually to have relaxed a bit. He speaks now, beyond yeah and great and surely, he's less anxious to please. Wonder what really happened last night? He said: 'Right. Guess you'd better come in about nine in the morning. Unless you're clobbered with an official function?' One thing's for sure—this one's not a pisser.

'No. My wife's got a couple of things this week, but I'm free.' Last week, there had been the mayor's reception when they arrived and various semi-official tea and cocktail and dinner parties arranged by local civic worthies. At only a couple she had taken too much; but not, he hoped and believed, so anyone would notice. Until last night. He had a fret that if the story of last night got around—Mrs Girdon-Ramsey must have friends, and she certainly had a telephone—everybody would suddenly remember small pointers and say I *thought* she'd had a drop too much, at such and such a soirée. Presumably the mayor here had some sort of congress with the mayor at home; and the mayor at home had the ear of the Chief of Police. They were not going to be very happy, if it all floated back.

'Right. See you tomorrow.'

'Sure. See you tomorrow. S'long, Al.' The young man left the office.

Jesus, Cruse thought with genuine shock, he called him

116

Al and got away with it. All the old sod did was grunt, quite friendly. He addressed Rosher. 'Come up with anything?'

'All clean,' said Rosher. 'Young Girdon-Ramsey's out of town with his. Touring. I'll check him as soon as he comes home.'

'Right.' Like every other policeman who was giving thought to the matter, Cruse believed that the wanted vehicle was registered and domiciled a long way from here. It might be local, but the races attracted custom from the big city and places for miles around. Lots of people professionally engaged with racing travel from course to course in portable living quarters. Cheaper and more convenient than hotels.

'Any developments here?' Rosher asked.

'Nope. We haven't caught up with the driver yet. All very quiet.' No need to elaborate, for Rosher. He would know about cruising police cars watching for a battered caravan, men at railway stations and bus terminals, calls by the city police on friends, associates, relations of the dead herberts, and at clubs and pubs where they drank. He would know about the other men, detailed for duty at every racecourse with a meeting scheduled. A seasoned copper is familiar with what happens, first stage in a murder enquiry.

'Uh-huh,' said the sergeant. 'Right. I'll go and type this report.' And he left the office where, in the days when he was Detective-Inspector Rosher, he sat cogitating over many villainies and tongue-bludgeoned many villains, en route now for a humble desk in the CID room and a bout with the hated typewriter.

Patrolman Hopper, meanwhile, was on his way home, walking through the fine weather. Not far from the station to the hotel, and the route is through the nicest part of town. Too much traffic, and purists say the square has been ruined by the new office block set, regrettably,

among Georgian and early Victorian shops, right alongside
the town hall built in 1649 with the inscription across the
top: 'So the eye waketh, let the hand sleep.' Nobody knows
what it means, but it looks very good up there. Bile arose in
purists, too, at the sight of cars parked cheek by fender,
packed on the venerable cobbles all day Monday to Saturday, except on Thursay, when the market was held as it had
been since Saxon times; but all agreed the traffic problem
was even worse before the new bypass came.

Again, here is advantage enjoyed by the American eye.
It absorbs without agony the high-rise new building, and
is well acclimatized to town centres used as parking lots.
Patrolman Hopper enjoyed his walk, any fret he carried
along coming from inside.

He enjoyed his homecoming even more. She was half
lying, half sitting on the living-room settee, reading a
book on local history which he borrowed from the public
library. Still wearing her house-robe, but scrubbed and
tubbed, with the dark hair tied back. Very young, dewily
virginal. He said: 'Hi.'

'Hi,' she said. 'Don't tell me—you're out on parole.'

'Time off,' he told her. 'I'm under oath to take you to a
movie.'

'Well—surprise, surprise.' She widened the big, big
eyes, in a hammed paroxysm of joy. 'What's on, if it's not
too sexy?'

'I don't know. I can ring and find out.'

She turned her eyes away from him, dropping the bantering manner. 'Jiminy, I'm—er—You know. I'm sorry.'

'Uh-huh,' he said. 'Don't worry about it.'

'I'm . . . You know. I don't know why I . . . It kind of—
comes.'

'I know. I know.' This far, he hadn't kissed her. They
had not even touched each other; but love for her welled
up hurtingly in him, and he said again: 'Don't worry
about it.'

'Present for you. On the table.'

He picked up the only thing there — a sheet of the hotel writing paper. On it was lettered, in big block capitals: 'I HEREBY RENOUNCE THE DEMON DRINK AND ALL HIS EVIL WORKS. SIGNED: ANGELICA HOPPER (MRS). 'The pledge,' she said. 'I'm signing the pledge, all legal and above board.' A returning edge of banter to her voice; but different now. Wry. Tentative.

'Well, now.' He grinned, to cover the almost tearful stab the child-jest gave him. 'I'll frame it. Hang it in the office. It'll go well with the puce walls. What sort of morning have you had?'

She grimaced. 'We weathered it, me and my Alka-Seltzer. You?'

'I been with Al Russia, the old boy I was with yesterday. Wait 'till I tell you.'

'Why don't we go out somewhere?' she said. 'Into the country, get some air. We haven't had a chance to look at it.'

'Haven't got a car.'

'We could hire one. Or there must be buses. Let's take buses.'

And that is what they did, riding into one of those afternoons and evenings when everything is suddenly right, and lovely. A bus took them through the beautiful countryside, threading lanes to the sweet village of Burton Richard (somewhere in England, surely, if a man looks hard enough he will find one called Taylor Liz?) where, trusting the assurance of a friendly driver and several travelling country ladies with fat shopping-baskets who nodded vigorously to confirm that a bus passing through in the evening would return them to town, they alighted and walked about. Great trees and a green with ducks, bordered by thatched cottages fronted with gardens a-glow with colour. *Vide* the purist again: too picture-postcardy, and the bloody place is full of commuters. Well, of course, it is; but to Americans it is the essence of Olde Englande, with a teensy touch of Walt Disney to help them feel at ease in it.

The pub opened, according to law, at 5.30. They knew it, they saw the man actually open it, and the lovable village drunkard lurch in. Hopper hesitated; and then he said: 'They sell bread and cheese in the pubs, out of this world. And hot pies. Feel like a drink?'

But she raised his heart high. She said: 'Don't they have a restaurant or something? A teashop—they have to have a teashop, don't they, they're drinking tea all the time. I'd rather have some tea.'

There is a teashop in Burton Richard. Two old ladies run it, and do it very well. Real cream buns and pastries, fresh fruit flans, thin bread and butter with homemade jams; and the tea comes in an earthenware pot, for pouring into good china. None of your metal pots and plastic. They charge, of course, my God they do; but Americans never really know what it's costing anyway, so this did not bother the Hoppers. They sat replete under the great whispering trees until the bus came as all those kindly people said it would, and burbled them back to town.

Dinner was good, too, in the hotel later, when she took only one glass of wine and refused a liqueur with coffee.

Afterwards, in their room, he said: 'Oh—I love you. I do love you.'

'Prove it,' she said. 'Let's have an early night, and you prove it.'

So they had an early night, and he proved it.

CHAPTER 9

Another character with sex on his mind that night: the Hon. David Lawney. A strange character, and still in love with his wife.

Correction. To say in love, or to use the word in any true and tender sense, is to pitch high. He was, after all, saturated gene and chromosome in the aristocratic tradition, youngest son of an earl, nephew of a duke; and no family reaps so rich a harvest in wealth and prestige and honour without centuries of cold-blooded whoring, of selective breeding, power to power, land to land, riches to riches. Ten centuries of it, and precious little is left of heat in the bloodline.

Occasionally, it is true, something hot bubbles, and a son marked for selling or a renegade uncle pants horny for a barmaid, a chorine, an actress; or a virgin aunt still unpurchased runs away with the under gardener; but the chins snap and the ranks close, and out goes the transgressor, portrait removed from the Long Gallery. There was not much love-ability left in the blood that gurgled through the Hon. David's blue veins.

But there was a certain heat centred in his sexual apparatus; and it goes without saying that the Blood, after ten centuries of dedicated greed, could not let go lightly whatever he regarded as his. This inbred rapacity, of course, explains how he came to be mixed up with that very shrewd judge of human nature, Mr Henry Croker. The lovely old house had a secret cellar in it, and a general layout very useful to Mr Croker. There was a stable block, and useful outbuildings, and the Hon. David farmed, or a tenant did it for him. All extremely useful — anything can be hidden in hay, or covered with a tarpaulin lightly spread with muck or fertilizer, and nobody takes any notice as it chugs behind a tractor from barn to stableyard, or anywhere else, for that matter. Nobody looks inside a haystack. Nobody can approach without being seen and look-outs can be posted, hoeing, raking, generally working in the fields. Nobody queries, either, the milk-float or produce truck leaving for markets in the big city, especially if the farm they come from is owned by the son of an earl, nephew of a duke. Two years they had been involved together since Mr Croker, backing his belief that a man intent as this one was on living in the outmoded style of his ancestors in this inflation-ridden age cannot be averse to tax-free money, made overtures that were not repudiated and moved out from the town to the house so conveniently bordering his property. Two profitable years for them both; and the next, the really big killing, soon to come.

Rapacity, then, rather than love, attached the Hon. David to the wife who left him, not because he beat her or had particularly filthy habits, but because his cricket and his rugby football, his hunting, shooting, fishing, and especially his birdbrain conversation bored her sick. She never quite knew why she married him, except that he had this lovely house and to marry the son of an earl seemed a good idea at the time. Having no particular respect for the marriage bond—watching a vicar from close quarters over many years is a fairly certain short-cut to religious cynicism—when it seemed a better idea to leave him, she left him. Still with heat in the loins for her, immediately he wanted her more than ever. She was his. What was his did not walk away. If she did not come back—nobody else must have her.

Of her earlier dabbles, with a travelling salesman, the estate agent who found her the flat she now lived in, and that bandleader, he knew nothing; but the boy Girdon-Ramsey was less discreet. Well, he had no idea that this was the Hon. David Lawney's wife, she didn't mention it. Not that it would have made any difference to him, except perhaps to add a certain piquancy. At all events, he pursued her; and from certain men of the farm who spent wages in night-clubs and similar places, word came back.

So he let it be known among the dubious staff filtered in over two years by Mr Croker that financial benefit would accrue to whoever brought the fellow in, having in his limited mind the idea of chastisement. Come to it, again, by the Blood? Always through the centuries, among the kings and nobles, if a man crossed you, you belted him. What the Hon. David did not know, then or now because Mr Croker played many cards close to his chest, was that young Girdon-Ramsey was moulded into the forthcoming little caper calculated to net no small profit.

And now—here was a mess. Two bunglers dead, and his wife come back to him all right. With a note.

He could see why Mr Croker did it, faced with sudden new problems and no time for solid planning. The girl was dangerous—if she went to the police, the mere fact that she was wife to the son of an earl, nephew of a duke, would be enough to focus attention, with reporters up here looking for comments from him. And if she had recognized Green and Harris and Chater . . . So: get her hidden away. A person could be hidden away here all right—one or two had been, as favour to Mr Croker. Friends of his, seeking cover before leaving for an unknown destination under hay or a cartload of cabbages. But they went into the secret cellar; and he had Chater there already.

His man Johnson helped him. Mr Croker's man, really, and a very useful fellow. He said: 'The small attic. She can yell her head off up there.' Because she was yelling already. Which didn't matter at the moment, with only the bent within earshot, but could later when the cook came back from her daily constitutional, taken in fine weather between breakfast and lunch. Cook was not of the bent. Unwise, in a country district, to change the entire staff in short time; so two sleeping-out maids remained, and the cook because she was so famously gifted people would wonder why, if she went.

'The skylight—' said the Hon. David.

'Couple of bars'll fix it. Not that she'd try it—too risky.'

Well, it was. Very steep roof with no coping, and a sheer drop to the cobbled yard below, with a horse trough right under. So Johnson screwed in two steel bars above the glass of the skylight to ensure that it could not be opened, greasing the roof below it; and he himself manipulated her, kicking and spitting, into the attic, where he made threats almost as bloodcurdling as those made to her by young Girdon-Ramsey concerning what would be done to her if she didn't behave. She'd be all right up there, having a rug on the floor, a truckle bed, a basin and ewer and the small chemical toilet brought in by Johnson when he had screwed the bars. These articles serviceable, if all but the toilet dusty. Maids slept up here once, when big houses were adequately staffed.

All day she was up there, and a very edgy day for the Hon. David, waiting for some kind of further message from Mr Croker. Late in the afternoon he sent—it was the man's own suggestion, actually. David had no power to send him anywhere—Johnson across the fields. That man managed a brief word with Mr Croker at the hedged edge to his rose-garden, and came back with a terse message. Hold her, pending instruction. Which did not help at all.

He took his dinner up to her, on a tray. This, again, was Johnson's suggestion. She'd had nothing to eat all day, he said; and as he, Johnson, attended to the serving, who else knew what happened to dinner once it left the dumb waiter? Go up, he said. Take her some grub and try to talk to her. Calm her down a bit, reassure her. I can feed you later, after Cook's buggered off.

So up went the Hon. David, with dinner on a tray, and he nearly lost the lot when she threw herself at the door as soon as he unlocked it. He managed to shoulder her away and himself inside, to stand with his back against the door, saying while he held the tray in one hand, fumbling to get the lock refastened from this side: 'Steady—steady,

old girl. I've brought you some food. Steady—steady.'
Lmited conversational ability, you see. He could have
been talking to a horse. Not entirely congenital, it is
educated into people by family and public school.

'You bastard,' she cried. Vicar's children are normally
less handicapped. 'What do you think you're doing? Let
me out of here.'

The fumbling behind had relocked the door. He moved
forward, tray in both hands. 'Can't do that, old thing,' he
said. 'Not yet awhile. Oh, I say.' The last because with a
whirling kick she knocked the tray right up in the air,
spattering him, herself and a piece of the sloping ceiling
with soup, fish, veg and Pêche Melba, and dolloping the
rest of dinner on the rug when it came down. Ballet
classes as a child. Not lost the looseness at twenty-two. She
probably wouldn't be able to do it at forty.

'Ow ow ow,' she went, hopping to the bed, where she
sat and nursed her foot. At some time during the day she
had discarded her fashion shoes. They draw the feet after
a time. 'Ow ow—you bastard, you bastard.'

'I didn't do it,' he said, dabbing with his handkerchief
at soup and sauces. 'You did it yourself. Very silly.' As it
was, with no shoes on. But a person does not always stop
to think.

'I've broken my toe,' she said. 'What the hell do you
think you're up to?'

'Have to keep you here for a little while,' he told her.

'What for?'

' 'Fraid I can't tell you.' He meant it, literally. Afraid
he was; and what was supposed to be her ultimate fate?
He couldn't hold her for ever.

'You must be bloody mad,' she said. 'Oo Christ—oh oh
oh.' She nursed her poor little piggy. The one that went to
market. Caught it an awful clout. 'How long do you
reckon to lock me in here?'

' 'Fraid I can't say.'

'You *are* mad,' she stormed. 'Think you can keep me locked up for ever?' Hit it straight off, she did. She had no idea anybody else was involved. Thought, knowing him, that he'd done this solo, for reasons of his own.

'Not for ever, no,' he said; and as he spoke she did a futile thing. She leaped, bad toe and all, for the door.

No chance of her getting through, the thing was locked. He did not even need to pursue her, but neither was thinking very clearly. He leaped almost as she did, arriving at the door virtually at the same time, his arms wrapping around her fighting body from behind.

'Lemme go—lemme go, you—you—' she panted.

It was the feel of her lithe, writhing body that raised the sex in him. Not really to his discredit, that it should. Four months celibate works in a young man, even one not given over to love. His hands shifted to her breasts; one moved down to cup the curve between her feminine thighs before she flung him back against the door; twisted to face him, panting:

'Yes—go on—rape me. Rape me, you've done it often enough. You'll look pretty, won't you, when I get out of here? Done for kidnapping and rape. You'll look very pretty.'

Not necessarily true, the things a woman will say in a rage. He never raped her in the legal sense. All he ever did was coerce her into yielding his conjugal rights, when coercion became necessary after the early days. Now he stood shaken by her vicious hate, unable out of his inhibited vocabulary to find words. So he turned, unlocked the door and slipped out before she thudded against it, on the inside. Relocked it and went downstairs, hands trembling, body tense with the stress of it all.

Two men without sex on their minds were Detective-Sergeant Rosher and Mr Henry Croker. To be sure, considerably more water had flowed under their bridges, and this can have dousing effect; but both were still capable. Mr Croker, indeed, enjoyed often the still buxom warmth of his wife, whom he called, in their more intimate moments, Pussy-boots. She called him Booty-boo.

Detective-Sergeant Rosher, it is true, suffered trauma that incapacitated him. He had thought at the time, shuddering in revulsion from women and all the danger they bring, that he was castrate for ever and glad of it. Lately, though, he had caught himself registering with approval the soft quiver of the town girls in sunshine, when they tend these days to unfettle the bosom, and the wonderful wag of hips as they walked. Never again, perhaps, would he know the old rampant roaring; but secretly he felt relief at the stirring; because the truth is, no matter how much trouble and grief that tacked-on limb brings him, after a long time of flaccidity a man gets worried.

This night, though, no woman was on his mind, unless somewhere in the deeps to which he had deliberately shoved her the brothel madam moved soft and subtly scented, as she moved still in his dreams. The controllable areas of his brain were involved with work, the way they always had been; and in the evening, having no inhibitions about ringing Mr Croker at home, he rang. When he came to an arrangement, he expected quick results.

He said, when Mrs Croker had summoned Mr Croker: ' 'Evening, Henry. What have you got for me?'

'Now, now, Mr Rosher,' said Mr Croker. 'Give me a chance.'

'I gave you one, Henry. This morning. Remember?'

'Mr Rosher, I am working on it. I have enquiries going on at this very moment.'

'That's good, Henry, that's good. Let's hope they come up with the golden rivets, eh?'

'They will. You may depend on it.'

'I hope I can, Henry. I'm known to turn very nasty,

when people make a deal with me and don't cough. You've probably heard. I really can be very, very nasty.'

Can be? You *are*. 'Have I ever welshed on a bargain, Mr Rosher?' said Mr Croker, with dignity. 'I shall deliver.'

'Until you do,' said Rosher, 'I shall ride on your back. And if you don't, I shall break it.' He hung up. Good exit line. Borrowed from young Alec Cruse, overheard saying it to one of his clients in somewhat similar circumstances.

Mr Croker also hung up, and then he watched on television a movie so old the long-dead actors talked in the voice of the Javanese Hoopie bird. And then he went to bed, several slugs of whisky inside to help him sleep; which he knew, left to himself, he would not be doing.

He lay in the handsome brass-framed double bed beside his warm wife, who nestled as she always had with her head on his shoulder, and worried. With justification.

A pretty pickle. A chain of events, right out of the blue, that seemed to become more tangled the more a man tried to straighten it out. For example:

What the hell else could he have done, short of having her eliminated (and perhaps that would have been best), about Lawney's wife? He had to get her out of police reach, and in some sort of custody. What else could he do, than have her picked up and removed to the only feasible place? Given time, he might have fixed it differently; but he'd had no time. And nobody had to tell him that at some date in the near future, she had to be (a) disposed of; or (b) let go; when she would gallop directly to the police, to spill about the boy and to charge somebody—her husband?—with kidnapping her.

Well—if they could hold her until after Saturday, all this would come later. After the big job, when he and his beloved (DV) would be gone. They could say what they liked, accuse whom they liked of what they liked, once he was safely beyond extradition laws.

She might already have been to the police. He had no

way of knowing. Couldn't instruct the boys to find out when they picked her up. They were just herberts, phoned in a hurry because he knew them capable. Hurry again—that was the trouble, no time for proper planning. The less they knew about why she had to be snatched, the better. Had they learned about her connection—and so, two and two together, his—with the red-hot matter of two dead men and a battered caravan, they might well have turned the job down. Worse—sensing potential for blackmail, they might have started nosing.

Lawney himself. An amateur. Very useful, the house. But you can't trust amateurs. What would he tell her? If he was prepared to beat young Girdon-Ramsey up because of her, he was still emotionally involved; and an involved man is wax in the hands of a cunning woman.

Was she a cunning woman? He didn't know.

Yes, he did. *Every* woman, present company excepted, however dumb is cunning. It's built in. He should have had her eliminated.

But how? No hit-men in the town. Plenty who would beat a man up, no questions asked if the money was right. Some—like those he hired—who would kidnap. But they would balk at murder. Time, again, the lack of it. It takes time to locate a hit-man in the big city—or in London, perhaps—and arrange a demise, when your profession, though bent, is strictly non-violent, so you don't know where they lurk.

Here was another rub: he was a non-violent man, a sensitive man. His own gut churned at the thought of murder.

His lady wife was speaking. Had been for some time. 'Rhubarb rhubarb rhubarb float.'

'Float, dear?' he said. 'What float?' Entire mind absent.

'You're not listening, Booty-boo,' she chided, pretty-pouting as even fifty-four-year-old women will, snugged up in bed with the right man. '*Our* float, of course. It wouldn't need much, in the way of changes—'

'Changes?' His mind sprang to attention. No changes to that float, if you don't mind, please. 'What changes, dear?'

'Oh, Booty, you can be *so* exasperating. Our Moolikins can be Britannia, all she needs is one of those pitchfork things—'

'Trident,' he murmured. Moolikins was Molly, elder of the horsey daughters.

'—and a helmet. And a Union Jack, she can wear it over the same Grecian gown she's wearing. And *she* can be whatever they call the statue on the Statue of Liberty. You know, the one with a torch in her hand.'

'Who can?'

'I keep *telling* you—the American girl.'

'American girl?'

'The one who's over with her policeman—he came up here.'

'Policeman?'

Probably with her head where it was she felt his heart buck. But she was frolicking on. 'O'Hopper, or whatever their name is. It's a *lovely* idea.'

Oh my God, thought Mr Croker: more complications. Because that float was built to his own design.

He had suggested, at a village meeting, that the custom be revived—it had lapsed because nobody could be bothered with the bloody thing—of entering a Hutton Fellows float in the procession which wended through the town streets in the wake of St Barnolph on a day that usually turned wet, once a year in honour of that holy man's founding the great church on a spot where he dropped his staff and lo! a flowery tree, just like that. Nobody remembered—unless it was the vicar—much more about him, but he rode through the streets on his commemoration day in a false beard and a bishop's mitre, straddling a white horse. And at night, many got stoned in the local pubs, which enjoyed extension for the fête. Many got stoned there every Saturday; but more on this night, because they came to the town in thousands. All very jolly, it was.

In the face of virulent apathy, Mr Croker undertook to choose a theme and design the float personally, to be constructed by himself, the Hon. David Lawney and the Hon. David's men, augmented by whatever village craftsmen cared to give a hand, in the Hon. David's stables. All the village had to supply was some virgins dressed to the theme. You find a few still in villages, but of course you have to catch them young.

Mrs Croker chose the theme, and enthused the Women's Institute and the Mothers' Union, in both of which she was prominent. The constituent of both, in fact, was almost identical, Hutton Fellows being a small village with a very finite supply of women. The Days of Wine and Roses. Moolikins on a throne, wine-jars (the Hon. David had plenty, in his cellars), wine-skins, virgins and Bacchus. Roses from Mr Croker, all over the place, and the whole lot mounted on a great, flat-bed truck designed to carry bulk from farms or wherever it happened to be. If the good ladies thought they dreamed up the idea, they were wrong. Mrs Croker did it. A lady of great skill in implanting into others the belief that they thought of it, while she smilingly went along, only for the ride.

'The float layout,' said Mr Croker, 'must not be disturbed.'

'It won't be,' his wife assured him. 'Only the dresses need changing, and the mound for the throne and so on.'

'I want the mound,' he said promptly.

'You can have it. It just needs redecorating. Hands Across the Sea. I can't think why I didn't think of it from the beginning, with them actually over and all this newspaper focus on twinning. Surprising that nobody else has thought of it. Perkins can be John Bull. I wonder if the young man would care to be Uncle Sam? They could sort of toast each other all the way along. Not liquor, of course, just the empty tankards—'

'No, Pussy,' he said. 'No policemen.'

'One can hardly classify him as a policeman,' she said. 'He seemed like a shy young man to me.' Totally illogical. That's the wonder of women. She added: 'And the girls liked him.'

'That has nothing to do with it. He *is* a policeman, and he's *not* going on the float.'

'All right, dear, if you say so. We can easily get another Uncle Sam, it doesn't matter if he's not American because he doesn't have to say anything, although of course it would have been better with young O'Hopper because of the newspapers. And perhaps you could make us a big golden eagle, to put up instead of the vineyard . . .'

She prattled on; and Mr Croker tightened his arms about her, all his worry shot through suddenly with love, and pity. He knew what it was all about.

She knew how he made his money. Always had, and there were times during their days of town living when she walked among the neighbours with her brave smile working overtime and her head high, after the local paper reported one of his infrequent appearances in court, shattering her assiduously cultivated façade of respectability. For two years or more she had known rest; but here it came again.

Here came stress again. Tomorrow the paper would undoubtedly report that he was walking about on bail. Bang went the courageous façade again. And she was no fool, she knew he would not have mooted and carried the resurrection of a defunct village custom, and actually worked on the construction of a float, all for the fun of it. She dreamed up the theme and involved the village women in it, as he asked her to; all for love of him, loyally asking no questions. She was a remarkable woman.

But she was stressed, even frightened; and as always, her mind took refuge in prattling, her longing for true, secure respectability fastened more desperately on the trivia that occupies the respectable middle-class lady with a respectable husband, living in a village.

He wished often, and more than ever tonight with his own fears and worries upon him, that he could be what she secretly wished he was—a stockbroker, or something as safe and stolid. But he couldn't, even for love of her and his two horsey daughters. He did love them. But: he was bent. He couldn't help it. Being bent is a kind of vocation. Or a disease. Which is the same thing.

Ah well. He patted her shoulder; and before his mind went busying again about his own worries, a new thought came.

Perhaps, in the long term, it was as well. Safe respectability brings boredom, and boredom brings dissatisfaction—even, eventually, hatred between spouse and spouse. Could be it was the element of uncertainty, of danger, that kept the love in her, in him, as fresh as the day when they met, he a young burglar making his way up in his profession, she a colonel's daughter gently studying art.

He had wondered sometimes if, very deep down, at odds with her need for conventional respectability, there was not a suppressed predisposition towards the opposite. She married him, didn't she? And sometimes in what she prattled was something that *might* have been a hint, a sort of guide, if he was sharp enough to pick it out. Like now.

A copper on the float was manifestly absurd. Perhaps she advanced that bit to jolt his wits. Because to have the wife there, logically essential to the theme: here was something close to brilliance, if she did mean it as a hint. Who would attach suspicion to a carnival float with a well-publicized copper's wife perched on it, dressed as the Statue of Liberty? And if his own wife approached the girl on behalf of the Mothers' Union or whatever—who would suspect Mr Croker?

He wished, now, that he'd never mixed himself up with the hard men in London. He'd been doing all right while he stayed with his own connection. But Lawney's house was so perfect for a clearing house, and the big idea came, and he had been tempted; and on his own, he simply did not have the know-how or the resources to bring it off. But once in with the big boys, you relinquished final control. Backing you had, and financial health after; but you were a hireling, a minion, and you could soon lose health of any kind.

And now, having planned and submitted the job, he was in to the ears and over. Without realizing it, he sighed deeply.

His wife said: 'Can't you get to sleep, dear?'

'Just a bit—you know. One of those nights.'

'Would you like me to get you something? A drink?'

'No, dear. No, thank you. I'm all right.'

'Pussy-boots knows what *always* puts her Booty-boo to sleep,' his wife said fondly, and slipped a practised hand through the front of his pyjamas. 'There, now—one step—two step—tickle under there.' God Almighty! Walkie round the bloody garden like a teddy-bear. Baby talk is one thing, but this is ridiculous. It worked, though, on Mr Croker. After a decent time of foreplay he mounted and rode, thinking as he grunted:

And Rosher. There's a hard man. He won't let go—he'll be on my back all the time, demanding information about that bloody caravan and who goes with it, and what the fracas was about. And if he doesn't get it, he'll lumber me for sure. Bail can be withdrawn. By Friday, I could be back in. And it's the boy's van.

I'll have to stall. If I can stall until after the job . . .

Oh—and the boy—the bloody boy—and dare I use Chater?

'Ah—ah—ah—ah,' he said, just as his wife rose up, rose up crying as the wave burst in her. 'Oo—oo—ooerrrrgh—ooo,' he went, and sent his own sweet bolt flying.

After a long time, she whispered: 'There, my love—there. Lovely?'

'Mm,' he said.

'Good night then, my Booty-boo.'

'Good night, my love.'

The boy. Where the Hell was the boy? The whole job went up the stick without the boy. He couldn't replace the boy.

The London men could, no doubt; but to ask for replacement at this late date meant revealing that something was wrong, all was not going according to plan. They'd want to know why and wherefore; and they were hard men, no doubt with an efficient intelligence service. Don't call attention, Henry.

Is she asleep, or just pretending? Please God, all will go well. I've got the tickets booked. She can be as respectable as she likes, for ever, when we get to where we're going.

Lawney's wife.

What the hell could I have done, short of having her eliminated . . . ?

Among other people of the town who lost sleep that night should be numbered the boy, Roddie Girdon-Ramsey. Despite the strenuous ministrations of the maid called Rogers, who shared (knocked out by now) his comfortable bed, he lay staring into the dark, held back from slumber by a set of worries closely inter-related with those robbing Mr Croker.

The van, of course. That was prime fret. What the hell was he going to do about the van? He had to do something—and do it fast, before his father saw it. His mother posed no problem. Apart from the fact that when she wanted transport she rang Riley, the chauffeur, and was picked up by the Rolls at the front door, never going near the garage—his mother he could twist round any given finger. She'd lie and cheat and steal and kill for him, he knew that. Like responds to like, and they were of a feather. But his father was a duck of a different colour.

His father was less besotted. Indulgent, yes, right up to the point of foolish; but basically, a shrewd man with a penetrating eye. See the bastard operate in court. Yes, indeed—a penetrating eye. Worst of all, he was honest.

Reason enough the boy had to lost sleep, in the fact of Saturday night's escapade alone. No way could that van be left where it was—tenants used the garage. The bay reserved for the Girdon-Ramseys, owners of the block, was walled off from the main cavernous hall; but even so, the situation was acutely dangerous. And his mother was not half-witted. At some time she must start to doubt, to connect the frequent newscasts and police appeals with his demand for secrecy, his huddling at home. Accept that she would never betray him—better, for all that, to have the thing gone before she took a trip alone down to the garage, just to check. No van there, she would blot right out from her mind any thought that it ever had been.

But his father wouldn't do that; and added to the tension was fear of what the old bastard *would* do. He represented terrible danger, the old man. Mother had induced him to lie, telling the Americans he was away, on Sunday; but that was when he believed that he, Roddie, simply preferred his own company to that of the guests. It had happened before, they told social lies to bores quite often, to excuse his absence.

A scarifying moment when, listening in his room on Sunday, the boy heard his father suggest that he run the

Hoppers home in the Jag. The Jag stood right by the
bloody van. Very dicey time, before the old man came
home; when all the talk was about the Yanks, pissy wife in
particular. Obviously, he had not seen it, or was so used
to its being there (but not covered. You'd think he'd have
noticed the cover) that it did not register. Most likely he
was preoccupied, getting the pissed-up biddy into the Jag.
Hairy, that was.

Not altogether surprising, that he hadn't spotted it
since. Wealthy men, like their wives, do not go into
garages. They are picked up by the Rolls at the front door
in the morning, and decanted back there at night. Even
the Rolls did not reside here. It went home with the
chauffeur, who lived rent free in a mews house. More
Girdon-Ramsey property. If the second (or third) car was
needed, it was brought round from the same place. Only
Roddie garaged downstairs.

And now, by God, he wished he didn't. What the hell
was he going to do? The luck couldn't last. And he'd com-
plicated the situation himself.

When Rosher called, in panic he told his mother to say
he was away with the van, up in Scotland. She did, he
heard her do it. And now, here was very grave matter being kept from his father; who had no idea the police had
called and thought his son was here according to normal
custom.

Lying now beside the breathing body of Rogers, he saw
clearly the whole cleft stick. Instinct said, on Saturday—
his first reaction—run. Foot down and keep going. But
common sense rose up and said: and how far will you get,
in a bashed-up van? Besides, they won't stop at this.
Whoever they are—drugs syndicate, found out you
pocket a skim off the top on every deal? One of the mobs,
caught on to one or two little help-yourself capers
employed when you worked for them? Who knows?—they
won't just sit back now. Second instinct taking over, he

made for home, and earth. Nobody could get at him there.

But now: he couldn't even go out. He'd thought of getting a quick ticket, flying away; but he'd no money until the bank opened, and this was Sunday. And no travel agent is open on Sunday. Not that he could have openly trotted to a town travel agent to beg immediate passage, preferably to somewhere beyond extradition laws.

By today the die was cast. He was stuck. Didn't even dare step outside the flat; because the police were cunning, they could be nosing around, and if somebody said they'd seen him, up went the balloon. But it went up, too, if his father, who inevitably met a lot of policemen in his JP role, mentioned in his ignorance of the Scotland story the fact that he was at home. He might; you never knew. Especially if one of them asked how he was enjoying his tour. As people do.

And Croker had been on. Well, he was bound to be, with the big job fixed for Saturday.

Or was he bound to be? Why the urgent label to the request for a call-back? This week in particular, the order was don't call Croker. Some change of plan? Or did he know what had happened?

The big job. Dare he take part in it now? Or: dare he pull out?

He couldn't pull out. People much bigger and harder than Croker had set it up. It was they, for whom he worked often, who put him into the job; chiefly because his skills made him an obvious choice, but also because he was local, and able to live here unnoticed, reporting on the (to them) unknown quality of Croker, who had marked planning and organizing ability, but insufficient resources and experience to carry so audacious a plan through.

If he pulled out—failed to show—they'd get him. He'd have them on his back, as well as whoever tried for him on

Saturday. They'd get him if they knew what he did on Saturday, endangering the whole enterprise.

I've got to get rid of the van, he said to himself. The van—I've got to get rid of the van.

And now he came suddenly upright, his brain saying: Of course! The only place. Why didn't I think of it before?

If I dare move it.

I've *got* to dare. Now.

He glanced at his luminous watch. Two in the morning. The roads would be quiet. Please God he wouldn't meet a police car. And traffic passing would see the off-side only, and that in the quick blaze of headlamps. Few or no pedestrians to see the nearside damage.

Beside him, Rogers had opened eyes just gathering wrinkles at the corners. 'Wassup, darling?' she said.

'Listen, sweetheart,' he said. The endearment stuck on his tongue. 'I've got to go out for a while.'

'What, now?' Feeling him move, her waking mind had hoped he was coming back for another piece.

'Only for a little while.' He switched on the bedside lamp. Smiled down at her, to mask growing dislike. He'd had her first soon after she came here, for the devil of it, and had used her as he felt like it ever since. Moving in to middle age, she was as besotted by him as his mother; and he had her in his bed now because she alone, apart from his parents, knew he was at home. The way to a woman's silence is by killing her or, if she has the hots for you, convincing her that you love her.

'What for?' she said.

'Just something I forgot to do. I'll be back in an hour.' He was out of bed, seeking his clothes; saying: 'Listen— lock the door behind me. We don't want anyone coming in, do we?'

'Who's going to come in?' She sat up now, in alarm. Women in surreptitious beds alarm easy.

'Nobody. But lock it anyway. I'll tap when I come back.'

That would insure against his mother's using her duplicate key, as she did very, very occasionally, to tiptoe in and stand by his bed gazing upon him as he slept. Or seemed to sleep. She couldn't insert the key in the lock, if his was in on the other side.

At five or so minutes after 2 a.m., with heart pounding in his throat he drove the limping van out from the garage and away along deserted streets. In the back he carried his runabout moped for use on the journey home. If calamity did not eliminate the journey home.

CHAPTER 10

So now we come to Tuesday morning, and yet another fine day. But not for all these worried people. Not for the Hon. David Lawney, stuck with his wife up there in the attic and the man Chater in the secret cellar. Not for young Girdon-Ramsey. Not for Mr Croker. Not even for his wife, when she set out in her own small car to visit the American girl in town. If the sun shone for them, it did so darkly.

Even through her worries, the Croker lady felt the impact of the girl's dark beauty as she sat on the brown settee in the living-room of this very nice suite, saying:

'I really am surprised the council or somebody didn't think of it. But there, I suppose they're tied up by red tape, or something. Anyway, we shall be delighted if you will consider it.' By we she meant herself and Mrs Gumsall, President of the WI and the only person she had been able to contact as yet. Mrs Gumsall was sure nobody would deplore a change of theme so cleverly topical, calling for virtually no alteration to the float. Even the virgins could wear the same dresses, and do the same things.

'Let me get it straight,' said the lovely girl. 'You want me to stand up there beside your daughter Molly, holding a fake torch and wearing a white robe and halo.'

'Not a halo, exactly.' Mrs Croker had a lovely smile. Purely good, all through. 'A diadem, really. And we can't have a real torch because of the children. And the fire brigade, I expect. I shall ring them to find out, but I'm pretty sure they'll insist on an artificial one.'

'And I ride along on a cart. Just like that.'

'A lorry, really. Yes. You don't have to say anything or do anything.'

'I'll do it,' the pretty girl said.

'You *will*? Oh—I'm so delighted. We all will be, when I tell them. Perhaps you'd care to come out on Thursday afternoon to our WI meeting. General discussion and so on. And tea and cakes, of course.'

'I don't know about that—my part doesn't need much discussion, does it? We're pretty full up all this week. Just send the clothes and stuff along, I'll wear them.'

'*Lovely*. How thrilling—and you'll look *beautiful*, if you don't mind my saying so.'

Why would I mind, thought Angie. I like it, because I'm secretly afraid I look like one of those bug-eyed bushbabies. Funny—I'm usually afraid of people, but I'm not afraid of you. You're all charm. And then, of course, I'm on the upswing.

The woman was rising now, and talking still. 'I'll have the things here in good time. Oh—and you'll need all the details for Saturday, what time we set out and so forth, although of course we'll send a car for you. If you need me for anything, please don't hesitate to ring, you'll find us in the book . . .' And so on, until the door closed behind her and the smile dropped away as she walked to the lift.

Mr Croker used the time, while she was out. He rang

Roddie Girdon-Ramsey. From a call-box set, rather oddly, in a nearby lane. Nobody lived close, so who, puzzled travellers often wondered, used it? Today Mr Croker did; and this time, via the mother he got through.

Roddie took the call on the extension phone in his room. Before the talk proper, he said pleasantly: 'You can hang up now, Mother,' and there came a small click.

Then Mr Croker said: 'Where the hell have you been?'

'Here,' said the boy.

'Why haven't you been in touch?'

'Rule, isn't it? No calls.'

'I've been ringing you.'

'Ah yes,' said the boy. 'That was a misunderstanding.'

'Why didn't you ring me back?'

'You have a rule.'

It was tavelling in circles. Mr Croker passed on to the pith. 'Are the police after you?'

'Why should they be?'

'You know very well.'

'Oh, that. No. And they won't be.' Hold the voice from quivering. Keep it casual.

'Your van —'

'It's gone. I'm clean.' It had been in his mind to tell Mr Croker where it was stashed; but now, voice to voice with him, he lost his nerve. If he was reporting on Croker, the old sod was probably reporting on him. He knew Croker had booked air tickets — the hard men told him that; and if he had all his future staked on the job, he might hold off for fear of wrecking everything. But he might not. He might report — he might even tell the police, if only for vengeance. Or he might panic, and scarper forthwith; leaving the job flat and Roddie stranded here. You never knew. That was the sod of it — you never knew. 'If I wasn't clean,' he said, 'they'd have been here. I'd probably have been inside.'

By the sound of him, the old man knew a deal about it.

Maybe he knew who made the attack. No point, anyway, in total denial. Croker wasn't asking, he was certain. He was saying now:

'You young fool. At a time like this.'

'How do you know it was me?' said Roddie. Perhaps now he would find out who he had to watch for. Croker had wide connections.

But Mr Croker, according to the wise principle of cut-out points and cards close to the chest, had no intention of telling how he knew. Girdon-Ramsey and Lawney occupied separate slots, neither aware that the other featured in the job.

'I have my sources,' said Mr Croker. 'You've made things very difficult.'

'How?'

'Don't ask foolish questions. You can't walk about the town, wanted by the police.'

So he wasn't convinced.

Well, he had to be. Sufficiently to keep him from talking to the hard men in London. Roddie had done a lot of desperate thinking; and in one way, he ran parallel with Croker himself. Get out of the country. The more he thought, the clearer it became that his one way out was to stick, if he could, to the existing plan.

It was all cut and dried for him. Flight clearance legitimately arranged already, as often before, for one light plane to Lyons. The isolated Brittany field ready, where he would touch down briefly en route. Quick hand-over, and take off again, on to the airfield at Lyons. That was the normal pattern. Only this time, from that isolated field he would just walk away. Concoct a story to feed to the men who took over the merchandise, and vanish. If he fed the right story—and that was no problem—*they* would vanish the plane. And he'd have a good start before Lyons reported him overdue and search was mounted. If they found nothing, they'd probably conclude he'd gone down in the sea. Just another unsolved mystery, and all forgotten in a short time.

He might even get his cut out of this big job. After all, he'd have made the delivery, and he could let them know where to send it when he was safe somewhere. Doubtful if they would; but money, for once, was not his main concern. Money he had from other jobs, hidden and never banked, because to plonk big money into banks is to invite query, and little things like lost interest did not bother him. Plenty more lolly, where this came from.

He wished now that he used his own plane, for these trips; but since he piled one, his mother and father both had vetoed another. With his own plane he could have skipped the job and run by now. Had the clearance time adjusted, and gone. But the hard men were in command. They hired the plane, or supplied it out of their own resources. He was given time of takeover and takeoff, everything planned and laid down to a tight schedule. Apart from the fact that he, the pilot, was carrying loot and flying on a false passport in a false name, everything about the plane would be legitimate.

So he had to stay in. He said: 'Look—I'm not wanted by the bloody police. They're looking for a damaged van. Right? It could have come from China. Mine's dug down deep. And they haven't been near—if they had a faint suspicion they'd have been here. Right? Stop twisting your knickers.'

'They'll be checking every van in the country—'

'Well, they haven't been to see mine. And if they do, I'm out of town with it. Nobody knows exactly where.'

'So you can't be seen in the town on Saturday—'

'I won't be in the town, will I? I'll be waiting at wherever it is.' He would be briefed on Friday evening. A quick telephone call, naming the place.

Beep-beep-beep went the phone. Mr Croker fumbled another coin in. He wasted most of the talking time it bought him. Isolated phone-boxes are all very well, but by their very isolation, anybody who does happen along notices more definitely a man talking in one, and what he looks like. And somebody was coming, walking the dog. 'All right, all right,' he said. 'But keep your head down. I'll be in touch Friday.' He hung up.

Tuesday is always a quiet day in the town, and it always seems more so when the sun shines, since the new bypass took away the lumbering trucks and other through traffic. Today it shone nicely; but of course, scratch any town and you find things bubbling beneath a placid surface. The everlasting human frailties, the hates, the violence, the villainies — they are still there. Dormant, perhaps, but only for the nonce. Every policeman knows it.

The police station, through which most of the hate and violence and villainy filters, never really sleeps. Today, for instance, in this town. Even to a visitor, or a bail-book signess, viewed from the reception area the old place would have seemed soporific; but in offices where the bigger brass congregated, brains nagged away at this case involving two dead men and a caravan, and a missing man named Chater. Nagged and niggled; and seethed with the frustration that often accompanies the start of a big case, when it seems impossible to proceed in any direction at all and there is nothing whatsoever to do but sit and try to think a break into being under the beady eye of the Press. Often, no break ever comes and the case languishes, passing finally into the files as open for ever, but unsolved. Sometimes it comes from outside — a telephone whisper, a man apprehended and talking, an EMTAD copping a culprit — and frustration gives way to vigorous action, with kudos all round. Much more rarely does it come directly out of those cudgelled brains. But a frustrated policeman must cudgel anyway. It's in the blood.

No particular need for Detective-Sergeant Rosher to cudgel. For one thing, he was no longer part of the hard core whose job it is to cudgel. Officially, in this case from now on he would operate at the foot-slog level, under direct orders. For another, he was off duty, taking the day in lieu of Sunday. But of all the coppers in the station, none more copper than he.

Not that he did much; but he thought a lot while he trundled behind the vacuum-cleaner and did all the weekly things that were meant to restore order to his house, but never did. And he telephoned Mr Croker.

'Ah, Mr Rosher,' said Mr Croker. 'Good afternoon.'

'Well, Henry,' said Sergeant Rosher. 'I'm still waiting.'

'You don't give a fellow much time, do you?' No ire, in Mr Croker's manner. Just the mellow tone of a man of breeding, jesting with a friend. 'It so happens I'm receiving a little feed-back. Nothing definite, you understand, but I hear there's a van with damage in the Hallgate area. Said to be under cover.' The Hallgate area. That's in the big city.

'Details?' said Rosher.

'I'm still awaiting them. You know how these things are.'

'I know how they *will* be, Henry, if this is all I get. I want full description of the van, the damage, registration number and driver's name. Right?'

'I'll do everything humanly possible, Mr Rosher. You know that.'

'Ay—and I'll tell you something else I know: exactly what I shall lumber you with, if you don't deliver pretty sharpish.' Click, and the ear filled with burring.

Mr Croker hung up and wiped his forehead with one of his monogrammed and utterly spotless handkerchiefs. Trouble with feeding false information to a man like Rosher—you had to follow it right through, and in the end it recoiled. Well—he had to be stalled. Just pray, thought Mr Croker, who prayed but rarely, that you can hold him off until after Saturday.

Rosher was ringing the station. Not much in this, of course, but he'd better pass it on. Chief Superintendent Fillimore, he asked for, and there was precious little warmth in Percy's manner when he said: 'Yes?'

'Sergeant Rosher.'

'Yes?' If anything, even less warmth.

'A whisper just came to me.' You couldn't say that Rosher radiated anything hotter than frost. 'A damaged van in the city. Hallgate area.'

'Description?'

'Don't have it as yet.'

Right along Percy's alley that was. 'Not much good to us, then, is it?'

Even at this range, and quite unseen, Percy could put the purple into Rosher's thick neck. 'Might be worth setting a couple of men on.'

'Where is it?'

'Hallgate area's all I know. Under cover. I'll pass details on as I get them.'

'Hmm.' Percy could not say outright what all his manner said: you twat, what's the good of telling us practically nothing? Instead, he said: 'I'll pass it on,' and hung up.

Rosher did not wipe his brow on spotless napery, but he passed his grubby handkerchief over sweaty palms, thinking how he would like to have those hands tight around Percy's narrow throat. Sod him—and I didn't have to report in, nobody knows I've got an arrangement. Seeing the handkerchief doing nothing in his hands he raised it to go through his high-decibel routine. All the motes and bits of minuscule fluff danced in panic on the dusty air of his hall.

Nothing else of particular interest happened on Tuesday. Hopper came home in the evening, that's all, after a day spent with the Panda Patrol boys learning nothing he did not already know, and heard that his wife might well spend the afternoon of Saturday doing Statue of Liberty on top of a carnival float.

He was pleased. Amused, too; but mainly pleased. A photo culled from the press showing her actively working on the hands-across-the-sea angle, sent to selected targets might go a long way towards countering whatever adverse reports had gone before. He said: 'Well—that's great. Who is this lady?'

'She's from the Women's Institute. Name's Croker.'

'Croker?' he said. 'Hutton Fellows? Is that the Croker we went to pick up on Saturday?'

'I don't know. You don't tell me who you pick up.'

He refrained from pointing out that she was too drunk on Saturday to notice if he had tattooed the name on her skull. 'It's only a small village,' he said. 'Shouldn't think it's stacked with Crokers. He's out on bail, if it's him.'

'She was a very nice lady. Talked with a mouthful of furry marbles.'

'Well, well. I'll check it with old Al in the morning. How long do you need to get ready, if I volunteer to take you out to dinner?'

He loved her all right. No doubt about that. He felt the familiar ache of it as he grinned at her, sitting fresh and smiling; saying in her comedy Southern: 'Why, *Colonel*— you *adorable* man, you jest *spoil* lil' ol' me. Jes' give me two minutes, while Ah work up an appetite.'

CHAPTER 11

Wednesday: nothing. Nerves screwing up, of course, all over the place—in the boy Girdon-Ramsey, in the Hon. David Lawney—when Johnson took her breakfast this morning she almost got away—in Mr Croker, who had another call from Sergeant Rosher and supplied a wholly fictitious registration number, saying his source was still working. Rosher himself rang the vehicle licensing office at Swansea to match registration with a vehicle. He hadn't seen Percy, who was out and about today; but if probing men were assigned to the matter, they'd fished up nothing as yet.

Swansea said the number belonged to a Ford Capri saloon, owner a Mr Roger Leonard Diccup of Jarrow. One of those things. Think of a credible car number, it's sure to belong somewhere. Nothing in this to point suspicion at Mr Croker. The sergeant rang the Jarrow police, knowing full well that ownership and car type would be confirmed to Mr Diccup. If the van was bent, it certainly would not be wearing its rightful numberplates.

Apart from these small matters, nothing of moment happened on Wednesday.

So Thursday came; and still no relief for police frustration. Senior officers assigned to the case were beginning to snap now at innocent bystanders. They always do in this kind of situation.

Sergeant Rosher worked the day mainly on routine paper to do with other cases—a burglary, an alleged rape—unencumbered by Patrolman Hopper, who went to the County Police Headquarters; sent there ostensibly to study forensic methods and bigger scale operation in general, but in truth to move him out of the way while others got on with the work. He was gone before Rosher arrived in the morning, and so had no chance to mention Mrs Croker's visit to his wife. Not that it affected any kind of outcome, there is nothing in British or American law to say that the wife of a man on bail must drop immediately any social or community involvement and step smartly into purdah. Hopper's viewing of it was purely as a matter of general interest. Which, again, doesn't matter at all, really, since he never saw Rosher to mention it. Pity is—because this would certainly have affected events—that his well-occupied mind did not register more fully a glimpse of a covered van in the Girdon-Ramsey garage, as he folded his wife into the back seat of a car on Sunday night.

Two telephone calls Rosher made. The first, as soon as he put the receiver down after the talk with Jarrow, was to Mr Croker, who broke out in cold sweat when he heard the undulcet voice.

'Your van, in the Hallgate area. It's a Ford Capri saloon, two-tone blue, owned by a Mr Roger Leonard Diccup, lives in Jarrow. So does the car, it's standing outside his house.'

Mr Croker had the point taken. 'Fake plates, eh? Yes—well—one expected it, really. I've been waiting for another call about it, before I rang you.'

'Let's tell your lads to pull the finger out, shall we?' No jocular use of the Croker forename. Old Blubbergut speaking, putting on the pressure.

'We can hardly walk up and ask who owns it, Mr Rosher,' said Mr Croker. 'Can we, now?'

'I'm not telling you how to do it, sonny. Just do it.' Another click. Another burring in the ear.

Mr Croker replaced the phone in its cradle. Worry, worry, worry. And two days at least before he could win clear.

Two endless days. But so long as he could stall, and provided nothing else went wrong, it would all come out right. The hard men in London had been most helpful, back when he had thought everything cut and dried. When he told them of his intention to retire from the country immediately after the job, they supplied really excellent passports and documentation in the names of Dr and Mrs Fisher. He'd seen them. All he needed now was to have them in hand, together with the briefcase full of money. The bulk of what he already possessed was stashed overseas by devious means weeks ago. What he'd transferred into the girls' accounts would enable them to live quite nicely, until—maybe next spring—they booked a cheap package holiday in Benidorm, or some such squalor, and vanished to join their parents. If they wanted to. He hadn't asked for fear of innocent prattle. If they didn't—and after all, they were big girls now, able to make their own decisions—all right, they could stay here. Nobody could touch them. And if they didn't know exactly where their parents were, even the like of Rosher—oh, a hard and implacable man—could not winkle it out of them.

Hang on, then. Hang on through the cold sweat, the sudden drying of the mouth, the increasing urge to pour bigger and bigger slugs out of the gin bottle. Eat in spite of the churning gut, to keep the strength up and to quell comment, for I am a solid trencherman. Pretend to sleep, for Pussy-boots's sake.

Sergeant Rosher's second call was made just after he came from the station canteen, where he had lunched off soup of the day, a meat and potato pie, stewed apples with the peculiarly thin yellow gruel that those who cook for policemen swear is custard, and two thick mugs of bitter tea, black from the urn to his special order. When the voice answered at the other end he assumed his most winning telephone voice, brownstone teeth bared in a smile above the gurgitation of gastric juices.

'Ah. Mrs Girdon-Ramsey?'

'Yes.'

'Ah. Good morning, madam. Good afternoon, I should say, eh? Ha ha ha. Slip of the tongue. Detective-Sergeant Rosher speaking. CID.'

'Yes?'

'You may remember I came to see you. About your son's van.'

'Yes.'

'We were wondering if he has returned home yet.'

'No, I'm afraid he hasn't.'

'Ah. Have you any news as to his present whereabouts?'

'No. We don't, normally. So far as we know, he's still in Scotland.'

Both her son and her husband, sitting at the polished table and eating off bone china food very different from what gurgled in Rosher, looked up sharply.

'Ah. And you still don't know when he'll be back?'

'No. I'm afraid not.'

'Thank you, madam, I won't bother you any longer. Perhaps you will ask him to contact me personally as soon as he gets home.' In the meantime, we'd better get kilties eyeing all the touring vans between Carlisle and John o'Groats.

'I will. Goodbye.' No name spoken by this lady, no addressing by rank. Not with hubby sitting there.

Mr Girdon-Ramsey spoke over his fresh salmon. 'Who was that, dear?'

'A friend of Roddie's.' His wife turned her eyes to their son as she came back to resume her luncheon. Not many people take luncheon, these days. The most they can rise to is lunch. 'I told him you are still away.'

'I heard you,' said Roddie, and not over-graciously. Nerves screwed up and still screwing. Nothing like it for making people snappy.

Mr Girdon-Ramsey was looking grave. Stern, even. Well-fitting teeth permit a good set to the jaw. He said: 'I am not sure that I approve of all this.'

'All what?' Mrs Girdon-Ramsey already spoke challenge. Not aggressively, but it was there all right, under the silk.

'I am by no means certain that I know everything going on.' Father looked at son. Son looked back, without expression. 'On Sunday we went along with your wishes

and told lies to the Americans. You appear not to have
left the flat since last Saturday. Unusual, to say the least.
And now, from what I just gathered, Mummy is telling
your friends you are in Scotland.'

Given a mother like his, a boy seldom has to answer
criticism from his father. She came in now. 'What are you
suggesting, Daddy?'

Mr Girdon-Ramsey knew only too well that quietening
of the voice, the silken tone of hostility. But, brave man,
he carried on.

'I am not suggesting anything, Mummy. But I do feel I
have the right to express my—concern. After all, I am
Roddie's father.' Still, when they grappled over him, they
spoke almost as if he were not present. Always did, right
back to when he was a mewing baby. 'If some mystery is
afoot, I cannot help but feel that the matter should be set
clearly before me.' Justices of the Peace, in tricky situ-
ations, puff up with pomposity as Gila Monsters inflate
their ruffs.

'Mystery, fiddlesticks,' said his wife, who also employed
a quaint turn of phrase during preliminary sparring.

Mr Girdon-Ramsey cornered a morsel of salmon and
speared it with cucumber on to a silver fork. He said:
'Lying to one's friends is hardly a practice to be com-
mended.'

'Oh, for God's sake!' his little lady exclaimed. 'Don't be
pompous.' In went salmon and was chomped immediately to pieces. She was annoyed with herself for having
boobed, in that she uttered Scotland. If Roddie wanted
Daddy kept in the dark, as often before, kept in the dark
Daddy must be. Just their little secret, hers and Roddie's,
as all the way back to dandling upon the knee.

Mr Girdon-Ramsey opened his mouth to speak around
very expensive fish. Then he closed it again. A row now
would only upset his stomach, he would sit on the bench
all the afternoon meting out justice with the gripes. He

couldn't win—when they ganged up on him, he never did. So he shut his mouth upon argument, using it only to chew right through to the cheese. Never for one second did he think of the boy's motor-caravan, and had he done so he would never have connected it in his mind with a van used to kill, currently being sought by the police. A man may disapprove of some of his son's peccadilloes and wonder sometimes about his secretive comings and goings; but it does not follow that he sees his own flesh and blood as capable of so violent a perpetration as took place on Saturday night.

There we are, then. No other relevant happenings on Thursday. Hopper and his wife spent a quiet evening and a happy one (because definitely the attack was over. She was bright as a bird and lovelier, and he a happy young man) watching, by invitation, a play performed in the town's Assembly Hall (built 1780. Rebuilt 1898 after the whole bloody lot fell down) by the Town Thespians. Sergeant Rosher moved among the pubs and clubs, ostensibly seeking whispers and keeping fresh his contacts with furtive little men, but in truth because a man on his own, fat wife gone home to Mother, has nothing better to do, the state television is in. Top brass grew ever more snappy, while rank and file didn't really give a bugger about dead men in a car, having more than enough work on hand already, thank you very much. And the world moved on to Friday, taking the town with it.

Friday was, if anything, even quieter. Shop assistants and office juniors found welcome relief from monotony in putting up bunting against tomorrow along the processional route. Publicans checked extra stocks, laid in for the boozing to come. Pickpockets limbered up their fingers. And eight men in two cars arrived and checked in to the Hopper's hotel, having reservations on the floor beneath.

Nobody noticed their coming. Plenty of visitors arrive

in the town's hotels on the eve of St Barnolph's day. God knows why, it isn't all that good. Nobody noticed their going out later, the second car leaving five minutes behind the first, or their coming back in. Most of these fête-day visitors take the opportunity for a drive around the lovely country, once the overnight bag is in and they have assured themselves that there are no bugs in the bed. Up Deacon Hill is a favoured trek in fine weather, to see the famous sunset.

This is where Mr Croker met them. Or rather, this is where he stood, alone on a pre-arranged rock until the cars arrived, almost together because the back marker made up time on the journey, according to instructions. Then he walked away, down a path that led to a discreet nook. One man from each car followed him, singly and sauntering. The other six stayed up here, in groups of three having no connection other than a shared interest in sunsets.

The two men came up soon, and after a decent time of pointing to features of the landscape — other visitors were here — the cars drove separately away. Mr Croker during this time was half trotting (you can't walk it, it's too steep) down the continuation of that path on the other side of the nook, to where his wife's small and unobtrusive Mini stood in the lane beneath.

He wished — oh, how he wished — that he was coming away with the passports, documents, air tickets booked in the name of Dr Fisher, and his cut-money all in his possession; but the men said no. Don't worry, they said — we've brought 'em all with us, you'll have 'em immediately after the job.

Don't worry. Easy for them. But he'd told Rosher, when he rang today, that the Hallgate area van was owned by a Mr Bernard Towler, who drank up like a man in the Pretty Kitty Club, Hagg's Lane. The Pretty Kitty Club existed all right; but to the best of Mr Croker's knowledge, Mr Bernard Towler did not. A big place to comb, the big city; but even now, Rosher might be ferreting out ᵗhe fact.

Well—it should hold him until tomorrow. That's all I need, dear God. Just let it hold until tomorrow.

Away, then, went Friday, unremarkably into history. On came Saturday. And Saturday, of course, was very different.

CHAPTER 12

On any fête day in any town activity begins quite early. There are floats in outhouses and yards and garages requiring last-minute titivation. There is the need to re-attach bunting come adrift in the night; this applying chiefly to official decoration, because council workmen are chosen carefully for their ability not to get anything right first time. There are excited children to be levered into bunny costumes and fairy costumes or whatever other whimsy adult fancy has wished upon them, and out again while late adjustment is made. There is a rush of morning shoppers, because only extreme foolhardiness will try shopping this afternoon, with the parade on, and crowds to be shoved through, and most of the assistants standing outside gawping. Even police stations come on lively, filled with personnel receiving pre-duty briefing before they tramp forth, uniform men to crowd control and traffic direction, those in plainclothes to mingle, watching for pocket-pickers, bag-snatchers, men who frot against close-packed youths or maidens and all who seek out crowds for their own devious ends.

Among the many up and doing this morning were the Crokers. Mr Croker drove quite openly to the Hon. David

Lawney's great house, in his own car with his lady wife beside him. No need for stealth today. Nothing more reasonable than that he, designer and part builder of the float, should appear with the lady who supervised its decoration, especially with the main body of the car filled with roses; some genuine, culled this morning from his garden to be carried by or pinned around the principal female protagonists; the rest of paper, fashioned by Mrs Croker herself and all the ladies of the WI, to fill the baskets of the virgins and generally add to the décor.

The float, mounted on a great flat-bed truck loaned by a road haulier who played golf and shot the occasional grouse with Mr Croker, looked rather good. At the extreme end, backing on to the cab, were skyscrapers. These were originally Ionic pillars, but a quick flip round with hammers, wooden boxes, saws and paint brushes transformed them very adequately. Likewise, the mound of painted canvas and *papier-mâché* over a base of even stouter boxes at the other end, originally Mount Olympus in the imagination of Mrs Croker and the Women's Institute, was now simply a mount, somewhere in America or somewhere in England—it really didn't matter, so long as it supported two thrones, side by side. The effect was pretty, all green plastic grass thick-sewn with plastic daisies, gold-painted thrones atop.

One of these thrones would know the saddle-toughened buttocks of Molly, the horsey daughter, every muscular ounce Britannia. The less calloused quarters of Angelica Hopper were to rest upon the other, bearing with equal dignity her country's honour, so long as the party was dry.

The rest of the float would be given over to roses; and virgins, who would wear, according to which side they sat on, Old Glory or the Union Jack sewn over their Greek tunics where the bosoms would be when they acquired the same. In their midst, two men: middle-aged Mr Webber, chosen because he had girth and whisky features very

suited to John Bull; and a thin primary school teacher
called Howley, picked for Uncle Sam on account of his
chin whiskers. All in all, a creditable turnout.

Quite apart from its main *raison d'être*, which had
nothing to do with St Barnolph's Day, the float had provided a second benefit. This was not the first open visit
Mr Croker had made to the Hon. David and his house.
On several occasions he had been up here for quiet con-
sultation and the personal transmitting of instructions;
but always discreetly, as encourager and overseer to a
working party of coerced husbands from the village.
Today, when David appeared in the great courtyard
where the truck stood now, brought out from the enormous stable, he beamed his benignity, watching his wife
and various bodies male and female clucking around with
roses.

Then he sauntered over and said: 'Good morning, Mr
Lawney.'

' 'Morning,' said David; and Mr Croker knew at once
that he had been drinking. 'A lovely morning.'

'Hmm,' replied David.

'Let's hope it holds for the afternoon. Should do, one
would think.' This he said aloud; and with a movement of
his eyes suggested that they should step apart. When they
stood on the edge of the patio overlooking the grounds
and farmlands beyond, he murmured: 'Everything all
right?'

'All right?' The Hon. David's voice had a definite slur
to it. 'All right? How the hell can it be all right? My wife—
you sent her—what am I supposed to do with—?'

Even *sotto voce*, Mr Croker could inject snap into his
voice. It took no great effort today, with his nerves strung
to breaking point. 'You will be told what to do. As soon as
the job's over.'

'I wish to God,' the Hon. David said, 'I'd never got mixed
up in it.'

158

So, by now, did Mr Croker. But mixed up in it he was and danger all around. This fool drinking not the least of it. He mustn't suspect that no instruction regarding his wife would ever come, that he would be left here to work it out for himself, Mr Croker many thousands of miles away. So the snap left the voice. It remained firm, but with a jocular overlay. 'You'll feel differently when you're counting your cut. What about Chater?'

'He's having breakfast.'

'Good. Good.'

Now Mrs Croker called, from among a knot of twittering women. 'Henry, dear,' she cried gaily. Very gay she was this morning, knowing now that whatever was happening, today was the day. 'Should we swag roses above the thrones, do you think? Or scatter them round the feet?'

'Ah,' Mr Croker called back, beaming, 'there's a question. Let us examine the problem.' Moving away, back towards the float, he murmured to the Hon. David: 'Easy with the drink. And we'd better not be seen muttering in corners. Let's get this thing down into town.'

Half an hour later the float left the courtyard, Johnson at the wheel, the Crokers following in Mr Croker's car. The clutch of happy women went home, having virgins to dress, lunch to prepare and jars of home produce to transport to the WI stall set up in the square. Ten minutes after the last of them left, the police arrived.

Inevitable that sooner or later they would. Unless the entire milieu is bent, and the guard constant, a prisoner cannot be kept in an attic for ever without somebody wondering. To place the top two floors of a house out of bounds is to excite the querying mind; and the minds of domestic staff are notoriously querying.

Had Johnson been in the house, the girl Edna (girl still, despite her thirty summers) would have stayed out of those upper floors, because there was a kind of menace in Johnson, and his word was law. But Johnson was out this morning, busy about the float; and Edna had reason for a quick flip up there, nothing to do with curiosity.

The fact is, she often spent unofficial time off in the attic next to the one containing Veronica Lawney, happy with copies of magazines bought by her brother furtively in a seedy bookshop—he still wondered what happened to them—and an interesting appliance purchased mail order from a firm who advertised therein and sent it under plain cover. She had been on tenterhooks since the embargo; because if they were about to redecorate up there, as stated, her little secret would be out. Her name and address were on that plain cover, and she a Jehovah's Witness. As, indeed, was her brother.

On this Saturday morning Cook, a puddeny lady totally incurious except in the matter of recipes, was in the kitchen. The second daily maid was away sick. She herself was in to serve coffee and biscuits to all these people fussing around the float. At an opportune moment, all served and Johnson out there, she galloped up the stairs with heart going bang-bang-bang. Books and interesting appliance stowed in her Jehovah's Witness knickers, she came out from her attic and was passing the door next along the passage when the handle rattled and a voice cried: 'Let me out—let me out, you bastards.'

Almost, she ran. This sort of thing is startling, when your nerves are on edge. But it was common gossip below stairs that something was going on up here, redecorating my eye; so she held herself and said: 'Who—who's that?'

'Me,' said the voice. 'Me—Mrs Lawney. Is that Edna?"

'Yes,' faltered Edna, knickers full of books and things.

'Get me out!' The handle rattled, the knob twisted. 'Call the police! I've been kidnapped!'

Obviously the door was locked. Edna tried it. Said: 'Just a minute, madam,' and fled downstairs, to jettison cargo and inform Cook. Cook said call the police. She wasn't a bit surprised, she said—where was all the food going, vanished out of her kitchen?

Nobody at the police station took the call too seriously. Heck, there were enough things happening. A call went out to divert a patrol car, more because when a gabble comes from so prominent a house it is well to appear on the ball than because anybody cared how the incumbent kept his wife. The girl on the switchboard, Inspector Blane who authorized the diversion—neither of them even knew that she was an estranged wife with a flat of her own. You can't know everything.

Ten minutes after float and titivators left, the Hon. David was helping himself to yet another brandy when this maid Edna tapped on the door and opened it, said, 'Two policemen, sir,' and vanished. Quickly. The Hon. David said, 'What—what—?'

They were very young policemen. One spoke. 'Good morning, sir. We're sorry to trouble you, but we've had a report. A lady. In your attic.'

'Attic?' said the Hon. David. 'What—what—?' He holed that brandy in one.

More seasoned coppers, wary of entanglement with the son of a belted earl, nephew of a duke, might well have drawn back; but these men were fledgling, still zealous in the belief that duty is duty; and sod it, the bloke was quivering, pissed as a newt and the picture of guilt. 'In your attic, sir, yes,' the spokesman said. 'I'm sure you won't object, if we take a look up there.'

Johnson should have been here. He'd have known what to do, they'd never have got through the front door without a warrant. But the Hon. David was an amateur, mixed in with villainy almost by chance; and he had known, had *known* with a certainty deepening over the days, that disaster had to come of it. Half blind he was with shock and drink; but even so, the arrogant blood gave one last kick. He managed to draw himself up, saying haughtily if furrily: 'I do object. I object most strongly.' And then little Albie Chater walked in.

He wouldn't have done it normally, fresh out of hiding, shaved, breakfasted and undisguised as yet in the false hair and other gear which he would wear for the job, because a bare-faced Albie would be an unacceptable risk, sought as he was by half the police in the country. Certainly he would have ducked back into his cellar had he known fuzz was about. But nobody told him, and like everybody else concerned in the enterprise, his nerves were giving trouble. He needed a drink, and he knew where drink was, having sampled brandy in this lovely room the night he arrived. So in he came. Too late, when he realized there were coppers, to get out again.

Zealous lads. The point bears emphasis. They had studied devoutly the photos issued to them, together with Albie's career record and all details calculated to assist in his apprehension. They knew him at once; and one moved swiftly the few steps necessary to cut off retreat through the door.

Both were suddenly very nervous, gouts of adrenalin pumping. A big thing for young policemen, abrupt confrontation like this. But they were good boys, they hid it very well. One said: 'Ah. Good morning. We have reason to believe your name is Chater.'

Poor Albie. Another man out of his depth. He thought they had come here for him, he fixed his guilt by turning in panic to the door; and finding the way barred, out of his mouth blurted the words he had used often and often before, confronted by sudden men in blue serge. 'All right, guv—it's a fair cop.'

So they put the cuffs on him, and the talking policeman turned to the Hon. David, who had visibly jellified. 'And now, sir,' he said, with a firm authority very creditable in one so young, 'we'll take a look in your attic.'

Three minutes later they let her out. She came livid and raging, as befits a lady forced to sleep nights on a truckle bed and squat at need on a chemical toilet, with no more make-up than she brought with her. 'You bastard, you bastard,' she screamed at the Hon. David when she saw him; and to the police: 'He raped me—he kidnapped me and raped me.'

'I think,' said the policeman with the speaking part, 'we'd better all go down to the station. Don't you?'

Detective-Sergeant Rosher was marked down to mingle. One o'clock his signing-in time, for a quite unnecessary briefing; to be on the streets in his black hat by two, solid among the crowds with his little eyes watching for the familiar tea-leaf, the quick pick-pocketing fingers, the lady fainting from the heat, the furtive fumble at a child, the obstreperous drunk. But signing in and signing out meant nothing to Rosher, and never had. He simply worked, having had nothing better, since his boxing days, to do.

He went to Hutton Fellows for a chat with Mr Croker; and this he did in his pre-duty time, because he reckoned a chat was due. The city police had been to the Pretty Kitty Club, which they knew well; but nobody in it had ever heard of a Mr Bernard Towler. He had no record with the police, and he wasn't on the electoral rolls. Nor was he registered as owner of any car or caravan. So? He could be an alias.

But Rosher did not think so. A seasoned policeman has a quick nose, unimpeded by thick hair in the sniffing nostrils. Fed suspect information by an equally seasoned operator, and fed it clumsily, he asks himself: why? And he sets out to find out in person because there is nothing quite like glaring eyeball to eyeball. Works wonders.

It was disappointing, when he got to the house, to find nobody there. He enjoyed Mr Croker, very nearly liked him. Always stimulating, to match yourself against a crafty old pro, and he had been looking forward to it. Woe would come of it, most likely to Mr Croker; but there would have been fun first, and the old sod should have known better than to try bending an arrangement.

It is not in the nature of a born policeman to leave the unpeopled vicinity of a known criminal's residence without casting around. Rosher carried certain keys. Many detectives do, very unofficially, together with pieces of wire and a strip or two of thin celluloid or its plastic equivalent. A french window is easy picking. He looked the house over, thinking the thought that must come at least once during his career to every copper surveying the luxury that comes to the reasonably successful villain: If I'd had the sense to be bent, I could have lived like this. Knowing nothing of the family involvement with a carnival float, he quite expected that somebody would return while he was here. The expectation brought no qualm, Mr Croker was in no position to shove a charge of forcible entry. In fact, the sergeant said to himself: I'll take a squint at the barn, just in case the old bugger's got a little something stashed. Then I'll come back here and be sitting in his armchair when he arrives. That'll shake him.

He went to the barn, and in the main part found nothing. As expected—Croker wouldn't be fool enough to use it again. But in the walled-off compartment where the huge haywains and harvest wagons once were stored, he made his electrifying discovery.

Nobody used this place now. A separating wall made it an annexe to the barn, entered only from outside along a track from a mildewed lane. The great door, quite out of sight from the house, had been closed for many a year, secured by wire that rusted and was replaced rarely, when somebody chanced this way and took the trouble. Rosher looked in on Saturday, just checking for a further cache, and found only cobwebs and a couple of aged rakes. Then the securing wire was twisted through its length, as is usual. He remembered untwisting it to obtain entry, and young Hopper refastening it when they came out. Now it hung from one hasp, doing no job at all.

'Hallo, hallo,' the apeman said, to himself and whatever bats, birds and bees chanced to be listening. 'Somebody's been in here.' He shoved the great timber door, using his powerful shoulder; and immediately added: 'Christ!' Because in there was the bloody caravan. And he only came to kill time.

No doubt about it. Scagged all down the side, nearside headlamp bashed right in, bumper seriously bent. No doubt who owned it — he had the list folded into his notebook. 'Jumping Jesus,' he said, and hurried back to the house, to use Mr Croker's telephone. This was approximately at the time when Angelica Hopper entered the bar of the Black Bull, and the boy Girdon-Ramsey came at last out of hiding.

CHAPTER 13

Angelica Hopper travelled to the Black Bull in a hire car sent by Mrs Croker to collect her, as promised. That lady could not come in person, the driver explained, she being in Dunn's Yard with Mr Croker, dealing with final floral titivation; but Molly the horsey daughter would be at the Black Bull, along with other fancifully dressed characters from various floats, all to be collected in good time with a stiffener or two inside to help them face the rigours.

A convenient and convivial gathering place, the Black Bull. Pleasant old pub, facing on to the market square. Plenty of side streets handy, where floats could be drawn up while the appropriate crews were mustered, sorted and mounted. Pre-parade jollity there has been a custom for generations back.

So Angelica came into the big, beamy and beer-scented bar, and was greeted by horsey Molly, who introduced her to several merry ladies and gentlemen in peculiar costume—she never did sort them out—and asked what she'd have.

Now Hopper, when he learned that she would be collected from a pub, batted his lashes and said: 'Well—mm. Mm.' She knew what he meant and said, being well on her upswing: 'Don't worry, nice old Jiminy—I promise I'll drink nothing but tomato juice.' And bless her, now she stuck by her promise, saying to the beaming girl with the hacking teeth: 'Can I have tomato juice without spoiling the party?'

'Of course,' said Molly; and hurried away, charmed by the way tomato came out tomayto.

There stood Angelica, then, radiant because her elated time was upon her, very lovely in her Statue of Liberty get-up, looking with pleasure on all these laughing, joking festival-day people. Not nervous at all. A little excited, but in the pleasurable way familiar to people temperamentally unstable at their times of confident elation. She was even prepared to go along with Hopper's declared belief that the British, when they finally gave out to you, were human. Charming. Hospitable, even. When the tomato juice came she sipped at it, chatting easily to Molly and the folk who gathered around them, drawn as are all small town people to the visiting foreigner, especially when she is in the news and lovely; and across the low-beamed room, Constable Wally Wargrave, due on at two o'clock and enjoying a pre-duty half pint, said to his oppo Constable Gordon Kenton, doing the same thing at his side:

'Oy—see who that is?'

'Who?' said Constable Kenton.

'The bird over there—she's the one the Yank was with. You know—Sunday night.'

'Wish I had his luck,' said Constable Kenton.

'She's a pisser,' his oppo told him. 'Pissed as a tiddler she was.'

'Looks like tomato juice she's drinking.'

'And the rest.' Wally Wargrave grinned his mischievous grin. 'Let's chat her up,' he said.

Had any senior officer other than Chief Superintendent (Percy) Fillimore been heading this investigation, it is probable that Detective-Sergeant Rosher would have stayed at Hutton Fellows, hidden with others in the barn awaiting the return of a Croker or two, if not the entire family; but Percy had these bitter memories, he feared the cock-up that seemed always to attend his efforts when Rosher became involved. True, the man was now a mere sergeant, and as such should have been easy to control by brass with a mind set on it; but Percy did not fancy taking chances. Not with this black-hatted git.

So when he was here and had inspected the van, and a plain car containing Detective-Inspector Cruse and Detective-Constable Oswald Mann was pulling up in the drive outside the house, he said: 'All right, Sergeant. I don't see any reason for you to stay. We're pretty stretched in town.'

This speech did not make Rosher happy. Not that he expected anything different. This was Percy, and Percy would, without doubt, shove him out of the case altogether if he could. And he could. Legitimately. All it needed here was a couple of men hidden away, the fewer the better. Croker was known, there was no identification problem and he was strictly non-violent. If he appeared—and Rosher thought he would not—a beckoning finger and a block on the drive to prevent his scarpering should be sufficient. Only after that would the forensic boys and general prodders appear on the scene.

No point, then, in arguing, and pride alone would have kept Rosher from it. He said stiffly: 'Young Girdon-Ramsey. Want me to call?' But he knew the answer in advance.

'Not necessary. It's been attended to.'

'Hmph,' said Rosher. 'Hrrm.' And as young Alec Cruse and his supporting cast approached, out came that great handkerchief. Everybody braced. Ritual over, the sergeant stumped away to his car without another word, for a savage drive back to town. Even as he was doing so, two police cars arrived at the Girdon-Ramsey residence and one went away again, they having missed the boy by a few minutes.

Also left behind was an almighty row going on in that sumptuous apartment, which came very near to ending with a well-respected JP strangling his tiny but popular wife. Appalled by his own potential for murder, he drew back in time and they agonized in separate, silent fear and mutual hatred; until, of course, the news was brought to them that broke them for ever. They hardly even noticed when they were charged with concealing a suspected murderer. But all that, of course, came later.

Rosher arrived in the station just at his official signing-in time, and found it buzzing, the Hon. David Lawney in for kidnapping his wife, the wife alternating between screaming rage and screaming hysterics, and Chater on the premises. An EMTAD was out for young Girdon-Ramsey and his Jaguar car, gone with him. He might be in town. Given that powerful engine, he could be well away. Unrelished complication to the task of policing the parade, upon which business the rank and file was already setting forth. Nobody gave him any specific instructions, so he went to the radio room. Nothing here of any kind concerning the boy. No call to announce Mr Croker's return and apprehension. He came out again, clacking along the passage to the reception area; and here he met Hopper, just coming in. The Yank said: 'Hi, Al.'

Rosher had the ill humour on him still. He grunted and said: 'What they got you on today?'

'Patrol,' said Hopper. 'Just motor patrol, see how things look out there. Just got back, town's jumping. Saw your old buddy, Mr Croker.'

'Croker?' barked Rosher. 'Where?'

When Rosher barked, the whitest of grins dimmed a little. 'With his float,' Hopper said.

'Float? What float?'

The American looked surprised, mind snared by a common phenomenon. Knowing himself, he had assumed that everybody knew Mr Croker had a float. 'The one my wife's riding on.'

'He was on a *float*?' What, had he gone bloody mad? Self-advertisement, with the van in his barn? No—no—he'd have scarpered, mixed up in that affair. Unless he didn't know it was there, unless somebody—Girdon-Ramsey, it had to be Girdon-Ramsey—lumbered him with it.

'Not on it—he was in his car. With his wife. Driving along behind it.'

'How do you know it's his?' He might just have been driving along, stuck behind it. Scarpering; but not rushing it. Easing away. But—shouldn't he have gone already?

'Well—it's got a banner. Hutton Fellows. And his wife called on my wife, asked her to ride on it. Statue of Liberty.'

'Where were they taking it? This float?'

Hopper looked more surprised. How the hell would he know? It was the job of the police, surely—the *British* police—to tab where the individual floats would park prior to the parade. 'I don't know,' he said. 'They're picking the people up at the Black Bull, two o'clock. My wife's there—she may know. Or somebody ought to.'

'Come on.' The Old Blubbergut snap. It worked still. Automatically Hopper fell in behind. As they passed the desk, Rosher threw words at Sergeant Barney Dancey, snug in his little glass enclosure. 'Get on to Percy, Barney. Tell him Croker's been spotted in town. I'm going after him.' You do it, Barney. If I do it myself, the bastard will shove me aside again.

They could not drive all the way up to the Black Bull. Streets roped off now, traffic diverted away from the town square. They left Rosher's car at the edge of the embargoed area and walked, some two hundred yards. By this time Angelica Hopper was elevated, bordering on drunk.

Hopper knew it, as soon as he stepped into the old-fashioned, liquor-perfumed, talk-and-laughter-loud bar. She stood in a knot of people, flanked by two young men, holding a glass of what looked like tomato juice; and her gaiety was higher, her laughing louder than it might have been. He approached, side by side with the sergeant. Said: 'Hi.'

She said: 'Well—if it isn't old Jiminy Hopper. The boy most likely to, given a chance. Smile, honey—you're among friends.'

Wally Wargrave spoke. No real malice in this young man, and less than that in his oppo; but they did enjoy setting up the piquant situation, just to see what happened. 'Hi, Mr Hopper. What'll you have?'

Gaylord glanced, and knew him. For once, no teeth shone out. 'Nothing for me, thanks.'

'How about you, Sarge?'

Rosher by now had heard the story of Hopper's wife. And he knew the pranking team of Wargrave and Kenton. One look, and he gathered the picture. 'On duty,' he said.

Up spoke Angelica, holding out an imperious glass like a little queen. A very lovely queen, many cuts above run-of-the-mill. 'I'll have another one.' Well at home by now, and in the how-my-people-love-me stage.

Wally Wargrave took his sense of humour, his wicked eye and the glasses over to the bar, where he ordered for himself and his partner a half pint each (good lads— you'd never catch them on duty half seas over), and for Angelica another of what he had been fetching frequently since the first time he took her glass: a Bloody Mary, but with a double measure of vodka. Pity, perhaps, that they ever raised the copper's pay to where young and single ones burn it up week by week. Your good old bobby couldn't afford to do more than grow crysanthemums.

Angie spoke now to Rosher. 'You've got to be Sergeant Russia. I'd know you anywhere, by your hat.'

'Rrrmph,' went Rosher.

'Er—Al,' Hopper said, 'this is—er—Angie. Angelica. My—er—wife.'

'How do,' the sergeant said. Looked as if they were right. A pisser.

'I do very nicely.' Slight sway on her. Slight slurring. 'How about you?'

'Er—darling,' said Hopper. 'The—er—float. Where is it?'

'I don't know. Why, have they lost it? Search me.' She spread her arms, mock-dramatic; won a laugh from the small group around. Molly Croker had turned from where she was chatting with her back towards them. It was she who said:

'It'll be in Dunn's Yard. It's collecting us at two.'

Sergeant Rosher was already moving. Hopper said: 'Er . . . Al . . .' The sergeant looked at him; and he must have liked the boy, because right through his normal utter involvement with the job in hand came the thought: poor little sod. Embarrassing. He'd better stay here. 'Shan't be needing you, son,' he said, and directed his square shoes away, out of the bar.

'Sure you won't have one?' said Wally Wargrave,

returning to find the Yank still here; and Hopper said: 'Okay. Thanks. Make it a tomato juice.'

'They sure grow tomatoes with muscle,' Angie told him happily, 'in li'l ole England.' It won her another laugh.

Desperation is what sent Roddie Girdon-Ramsey out on to the streets, five or so minutes before the police came to tell his parents—his mother, at first asking, insisted that he was still in Scotland—that his van had been found hidden at Hutton Fellows and was almost certainly the one that killed two men last Saturday. Sheer, unalloyed desperation. If the man who rang him had known that he was already wanted by the police—well—he would never have rung, in the first place. Hard to say what he would have done. Contacted the hard men in London, perhaps, seeking guidance.

And what would they have done? Called the job off? Woe betide young Girdon-Ramsey, if they'd had to. Woe betide him in any case, so far as he could see when the call came, if he didn't get out of England. Oh yes.

The man who rang was called Eddie Langdon, and he was in command of the bunch of men who arrived yesterday in two cars. All the planning was done, everything cut, dried and confirmed as being in apple-pie order by Mr Croker during that little chat of last evening in a dell near the crest of Deacon Hill. So the men boarded their cars this morning, driving to where they had to be; and bloody Chater didn't turn up.

They did not even know that his name was Chater, they certainly didn't know he'd been arrested or anything about him. All they knew was: a local man should have been there to guide them unerringly when the initial job was done to Dunn's Yard. And he didn't turn up.

Now they couldn't afford to hang around for long. Planning was meticulous, time of the quarry's arrival all arranged. No problem, the job itself. But—no guide? Sod that. They'd never seen the bloody town before. The loot had to vanish, fast, transported to the right place. No, they couldn't muck about.

Well: Eddie had two phone numbers only to ring in case of emergency. He tried the first, and drew blank. Mr Croker was already gone. So he rang the second, given to him as belonging to the boy more or less representing the hard men in this area. Mrs Girdon-Ramsey took the call.

He said: 'Hallo. Who's that?'

'The name,' she said, 'is Girdon-Ramsey.'

'Oh. Rodney Girdon-Ramsey?' Daft question? Maybe. But there are men who speak between mezzo and contralto. After all, Eddie never met the boy. Be fair.

'He is my son. Do you wish to speak to him?'

There you are. Another daft question. Eddie would hardly have been incarcerated in a little red booth with a sweaty phone clasped to his ear if he didn't. He said: 'Yeah. Thass right.'

'Whom shall I say is calling?'

'Just tell him his friends from London.'

'Just a moment.' She laid the receiver down and made for the stairs up to the room where Roddie was spending all his time now, apart from the little it took to consume meals. And some of these he missed. But not many, for fear of exacerbating whatever suspicion lurked in his father; who was here now, no court sitting on Saturday. He looked up from his paper and cocked an eyebrow. His wife said: 'Friends'; and she travelled on.

When she came back, he said: 'Friends? What friends?'

'Roddie's friends,' she said, 'are Roddie's own affair.'

He put aside his paper, saying: 'Mummy, I demand to know what's going on. The boy hardly comes out from his room—'

She bore him down, all the danger signals flying. They show in the eyes, in the stiffening body, in the way a telephone receiver is replaced in its bracket. They show in the crackling voice. 'Roddie's movements are also his own affair. He needs rest, he's been working hard.'

Ridiculous. The boy never worked hard at anything in his life, and his father knew it. But you'll get no sense from a fixated mother, all you'll get is trouble. So Mr Girdon-Ramsey glared back at his wife's glare; made a sound like grrumph and erected his paper again. Simmering silence came between them.

Upstairs, there was talking. Roddie, nerves shredded and reshredded by a week of tension that had mounted to panic since he realized the fool thing he had done, almost keeled over when his mother gave the message. O my Christ—was it all tumbled?

The conversation was brief. Eddie was not here to chat. He said: 'Your geezer. Your guide. He ain't arrived.'

'Ah,' said Roddie.

'Where is he?'

'I—I—X fixed him.' X stood for Croker.

'Rung him. Nobody there. Listen—we can't hang about. You know this town?'

'Yes.' Oh, thank God—the call was not as he feared.

'You know the exchange point? This yard?'

'Yes.'

'Get out here. You know where we are.' Click went the phone and Eddie was gone before Roddie could frame the words: 'I—I—I can't. I can't come out in the town.'

The boy's hands needed two shots at getting the receiver back in its nest. He couldn't go out—he couldn't. On the other hand—he couldn't not. He *must* go.

When his mother arrived to announce the call, his near fainting came at first from the conviction that it had happened, the thing he knew would, since the euphoria died after he rid himself of the van. Croker had found it. It was a crazy place to put it, a straw-clutch born of desperation; and he had lived with mounting terror ever since the cold facts insisted on recognition.

He must have been out of his mind. It was his father's fault—it was all his father's fault. If it hadn't been for his father the thing could have stayed where it was, at least until he'd been able to contact people who would dispose of it.

But what people? He didn't know who came gunning, he didn't know whom he dared contact. A whisper circulating that he and the van were here, a grass currying favour or making a few bob from the fuzz . . . Or the gunning bastards might come again. Whoever they were.

One thing for sure: the hard men would get him if they knew what he'd done; and there are worse ways to die than by gunshot.

Where was fucking Chater?

If the job went wrong—they'd blame him, Roddie. They'd get him.

He had to get away—out of England, in that plane. But the only way to the plane was according to plan. The job done, and the loot with him. The job gone wrong, the plane would be whisked away. Or never sent—because most likely (he didn't know; all he knew of the set-up was what they allowed him to know) the hard men would wait for a phone whisper saying all's well before they nodded it away. They wouldn't want it standing for hours, conspicuous on that small airfield, until he arrived to take it over.

He *had* to get away. Or perish.

What was fucking Croker up to? Where was this guide?

He'd have to do it. He'd *have* to. He couldn't even ring that London bastard back. And the bastard had given orders on behalf of the hard men.

You could not call it courage, then, his venturing forth. Desperation. Pure desperation. And do you know, this lad was so bent that even as he left the apartment—by the back door, bypassing his parents altogether—the thought began to whisper in his mind, somewhere under his clamouring fear: Maybe I can scrub the Brittany field, fly on somewhere. Keep all that loot for myself.

A man must be vocationally bent for such a thought to whisper at such a time. Five minutes later came the police.

Mr Croker stood with his wife in Dunn's Yard, putting finishing touches to the float décor. Erecting the banner and rearranging roses was about the sum of it, nothing else left to do; but sheer tension kept them from relaxing, as Johnson seemed to be doing. If they had asked him to sit up on the cab seats instead of lying stretched across, they could all have perched quite comfortably side by side. Nothing to pass the time, though, except to stare through the windscreen at the great doors fronting on to Calum Street, through which the float would trundle in time en route for the parade.

Johnson's lounging in the cab at least kept him out of earshot. Which was not all that important, since what Mr Croker needed to say to his wife was said on the way here, as they drove in his car behind the float. A very brief briefing, it was. He merely said: 'Darling—will you trust me?'

'Yes,' she said. 'Of course.' But her heart leapt cold in her breast like a flutter of fly-catching minnows. Her voice was quiet, her hands even managed not to jump up to her mouth. But her eyes were very, very frightened.

'Good. Then I'd like you to change plan a little. As soon as the parade is done I'd like you to make excuses—skip the celebrations and so on. Will you do that? Go home immediately the parade finishes?'

'If you want me to, dear.'

'Thank you, my love. And—er—pack a case. Will you? Just a few things—clean underwear and so on. Shirts. We'll buy what we need when we get there. Just pack a small case and wait for me.'

A remarkable woman. Not unique—many women, loving a man, ask no questions whatever he does. But these are normally besotted; and she was not, really. She loved him—without any doubt, theirs was a true love-match—but how could she, living all these years with him, not view him with open eyes? And yet she made no fuss. Perhaps love's empathy told her that whatever he was up to was designed to relieve them both for ever from the financial pressure that kept him cobbling. All criminals dream of the big one that will free them ever more from their craft; and often, knowing nothing less will wean them away, their wives come to dream of it too. She did not even ask where they were going. She said, merely: 'All right, dear.'

Now, fiddling with roses massed on the float, he spoke softly. 'You know what to do, dear, don't you?'

'Yes,' she said, and after hesitation: 'Henry—I—be careful, my love.'

'Trust me,' said Mr Croker. Unusually husky tone. 'Will you trust me, Pussy-boots? I love you. You know that. What I'm doing is for both of—' And he broke off; because the second set of huge doors, the ones through which the float entered the yard from the cobbled, scrap-yard-bordered area behind this great, old warehouse building, was opening and a known figure in a black hat was coming through. At its heels trod a uniform police-man.

'Ah,' said Rosher. 'Henry.'

Mr Croker clothed his face with affability, his voice in heartiness. 'Well—Mr Rosher. What brings you to these parts?'

'You do, Henry,' said Rosher. 'We've come for you. Can you guess why?'

Mr Croker was sure that he could. He had no knowledge of the Hon. David's arrest, or of the nobbling of Chater; but something had gone wrong. The job was blown, the police knew. Gamely he kept the heartiness glowing. 'I'm not very good at guessing games. Am I, dear?'

'No,' said his wife.

'I'll give you a clue.' Rosher, too, was wreathing himself in affability. 'A caravan. A motor-caravan.'

'What motor-caravan?' asked Mr Croker, and received a spectacular shock.

'The one we've been looking for, Henry. Property of one Rodney Girdon-Ramsey. Just to think — it was in your barn all the time. Wasn't it?'

A man coping with one shock is knocked all sideways by another dealt from a totally unexpected angle on a different issue. 'Van?' said Mr Croker, heartiness suddenly gone. Goggling eyes and a yellowish skin-glisten replaced it. 'Barn? What van? What barn?'

'Come along, lad,' Rosher said. 'Let's be having you.'

The creaking of the great door, the sudden voices, had sat Johnson up on his seat. He was thinking: Christ — coppers; and to him came the sudden need to be gone. But he never had a chance. Rosher saw him, and said: 'Hallo, hallo — who are you?'

Johnson should have said: Me? I'm just the bloke who drives the float. He might have been left there, unmolested. But rising panic had him reaching automatically for a cover of extreme rectitude. Like Mr Croker, he knew nothing of earlier police activity; so he said with dignity: 'I am Mr Johnson. The Honourable David Lawney's personal gentleman.'

'Are you, bechrist?' said Rosher, very pleased indeed. 'Well — your boss is nicked. You'd better come with us.' And crisply to the uniform man, as Johnson made as if to descend hurriedly from the cab with a view to fast running: 'Hold him, Ernie. Better put the cuffs on him. I think we'd better have 'em on you, too, Henry. And you'd better come along, Mrs C.'

Easy. So easy. But you see, all except the coppers were taken completely by surprise; and how would they dare stay to argue, knowing what would have equally surprised the policemen: that a truck filled with loot would arrive very shortly—if the time plan held, in a matter of minutes?

So a little bundle of people left Dunn's Yard with the float still standing in it, and shuffled along to the police car left some distance away, so the noise of an approaching engine would not raise alarm. Last one out, the uniform man tidily refastened the padlock securing the great wooden doors.

The hair bristled on Roddie Girdon-Ramsey's neck, the fear dried his mouth, churned his bowel, almost blinded him as he drove in that conspicuous car through the town, by back streets away from the bunting area, across country to a lane where a dirt road led through a wood to a tumbledown farm, long abandoned. He turned on to this road, and when he reached the farmyard one of the men from London stepped out from the roofless house and pointed to the Jag. 'Get that fucking thing under cover,' he ordered. 'Over there—in the barn.'

Roddie moved the car on. As he approached the almost unhinged barn doors they opened, shoulder-shoved by two more men, both dressed as coppers. More men in here, some in the uniform, some in plain clothes; and two cars, one of them garishly piebald to match the panda cars used by the local police. Very easy job, and quick, to pandarize an all-black car. Thin self-adhesive plastic panels in white, shaped from the stuff you use on kitchen tables and the like. Five minutes to smooth them on. Twenty seconds to rip them off later and away you go, cruising in an innocuous black saloon. Provided nobody gets up close enough to poke, it works a treat.

Gaining the shelter of the barn brought the boy no

comfort. None of these men was known to him, but they looked a hard bunch. God help him. It flashed into his mind that they knew about everything, that they had lured him here for elimination before they drove away, the job abandoned. But no—they were geared up and waiting. One of the plain-dressed characters spoke briefly. Nobody else did—they were all staring at him. Hard eyes.

'He's here, Eddie.'

Eddie Langdon knew very well that he was here. A Jaguar cannot drive into a fusty, dusty, cobwebby old barn unnoticed by a reasonably alert somebody inside. He looked up from a portable radio receiver and said: 'Where's your fucking geezer?'

'I don't know,' the boy replied; and in case this little speech sounded like couldn't-care-less repudiation of responsibility: 'I wasn't fixing him—he belongs to X.'

'I know who he fucking belongs to.' Eddie was snappy. Criminals engaged upon an enterprise hate the unforeseen, it makes them edgy. From the start he had misliked the matter of being out of possible contact with Mr Croker from when that man left home on the morning of the job. Now he misliked it more than ever. Mind you, it made sense for Mr Croker to be walking about clean, no radio crackling and gobbling on his person. Even so, it had him edgy. He just had time to say: 'Well, I hope you know the fucking town,' before his receiver spoke. It said chilli con carne. Quails in aspic, Eddie told it, and switched off. To men already on the move he said: 'All right, boys—let's go.' And to Roddie: 'None too fucking early, was you? You travel in the Viva, with me.'

A short time after the two cars drove away from that tumbledown farm Mr Malcolm Bootey arrived at Dunn's Yard. Mr Bootey was the regular driver of the flat-bed truck upon which the float was mounted, a Heavy Goods Vehicle driving-licence holder happy to pick up a fair gratuity, permission of the boss, Mr Dunn, for driving it this Saturday afternoon in the parade. When he came into the yard by a small door inset in the Calum Street entrance, he said: 'Funny. Where is everybody?' Because he had understood there would be somebody here, waiting.

He mounted to the familiar cab and smoked a cigarette; saying as he stubbed the butt: 'Well—buggered if I know—am I supposed to go, or what?' Heavy Goods drivers in their lonely cabs tend to talk to themselves. It keeps them from going mad. A few more minutes and he said: 'I must have got it wrong, they must have meant somebody'd meet me at the Black Bull. Anyway, if I don't move out they'll miss the bleeding parade altogether. One thing—if they come here looking for me, they'll know where to find me.' He reached down to the knob of the heavy duty starter motor.

No organizer was with him, then, when the float drew up close by the Black Bull, six others here before him. He had to leave the truck, rooting the crew out from the bar himself. The copper on duty said yes, it'll be all right here, as long as you're not too long; and he was not. Only as long as it took to sink a proffered pint; during the act, thinking: The Statue of Liberty, or whatever she is—she's well pissed.

He did her no great injustice. The mischievous duo, Wargrave and Kenton, had enjoyed a little fun and gone their way, uniforms in holiday holdalls, to be donned at the station.

With a deal of talk and laughter the fancy-dressed people were quitting the bar, separating outside to find whichever of the floats they were garbed to adorn. Among them went the Statue of Liberty girl, one arm held by an unsmiling young man called, if Mr Bootey heard it right, Jiminy Cricket. As he swallowed the last of his pint, thinking he'd better be there to see them all aboard, a horsey-looking girl dressed as Britannia came up and said: 'Where are my mother and father?'

'Pardon?' he said.

'My parents. Mr and Mrs Croker. Weren't they supposed to be with you?'

'Nobody arrived, dear. I thought somebody was going to be in the yard, but they wasn't. So I brought it along.'

'Oh well,' said Molly, 'no doubt they'll catch us up.'

CHAPTER 14

This was the nerve-racking part of the job for the men involved: driving that pseudo-panda car half a mile along the bypass from where the lane from the farm joined it; stationing it broadside to block the eastbound carriageway; piling out in police uniform to erect diversion signs and flag down traffic as it came along, waving it with the aplomb of real policemen and all the standard point-duty gestures down yet another lane; at a small off-turn from which stood another arrowed sign, another uniform, to keep it on the main lane; which would return it to the bypass out of sight round a bend from where it went in. If a motorist asked questions he would be told that an accident had happened, blocking the bypass where he couldn't see it, other side of that bend. Very simple. But a time of danger.

Suppose, for example, that a genuine patrol car came along, and the crew got out to assist or/and ask pertinent questions, having heard nothing about hold-ups on this, their stretch of the bypass. Awkward. Especially if they approached along the other carriageway. No good at all telling them of road blockage beyond a bend round which they had just motored. This danger was minimized by the fact—it was one reason why today was the chosen day—that the police were stretched beyond capacity back there in the town. Even so, there was no denying the danger. Oh, the unlucky coppers would have been dealt with, all these men carried coshes, and pistols too; but it is dicey, coshing coppers before the surprised eyes of passing motorists, and the man who shoots one is mug indeed. Nothing to do, a copper shot, but leap into the nearest car to vanish in a squeal of tyres; and there goes the job, blown.

No contretemps today, the whole operation took no more than three or four minutes. That chilli con carne message came from a man stationed to report when the truck passed a certain point. Mr Croker's time-plan was working beautifully. A dozen motorists diverted, and here it came.

Not an enormous truck—more a large-sized van, two men on motor-bikes riding before, two more behind. Obedient to direction, they all turned into the lane. One of the policemen held up the following traffic; the others moved back to the car, taking their diversion signs with them. The tarted panda reversed, paused to pick up that last man and drove in the wake of the quarry. The traffic flowed on along the bypass. Simple, and very smooth. A few more minutes and this particular squad could rip the white plastic off and drive away, their task finished. They would not even know what was in the truck. They were here purely on contract.

At about this time, the police station rocked. Not visibly, but a psychic observer, tuned in, would have reeled at the impact. The Hon. David Lawney, drunk and close-questioned, implicated Mr Croker in the kidnapping of his wife; and with this point leaped upon by Detective-Inspector Bomber Bates, a good man at harrying, he burbled on bit by bit until all he knew of the big job—it wasn't very much, apart from the fact that it must be taking place about now, or very shortly—lay revealed. Furthermore, sobbing through a combination of hell-fury and hysterics, the kidnapped wife confirmed Roddie Girdon-Ramsey as driver of last week's killer van only this morning come to light, and as threatener of acid bath for her delicate skin.

On a day of general knees-up, an eruption like this is all a policeman needs. Truly, his cup runneth over. The Chief Constable took personal charge. He was here already, of course; but keeping in the background, as a good leader should at a time of routine activity. Now he was suddenly much more here, holding emergency office consultations with Detective Chief Superintendent (Percy) Fillimore, back from Hutton Fellows now that Croker was netted, and Chief Superintendent Rolly Rawlins, little king of the uniform branch.

Impossible situation, really, no matter who was in charge. All the Hon. David could tell them was that something was happening. He didn't know what. Whatever it was, it was happening in town. When he got this far he suddenly clammed up, saying nothing about the float. But he did imply that Mr Croker set it all up.

Time was passing. Time was passing. The Chief standing by, Percy got down to the task of cracking Mr Croker. But Mr Croker was a wily old pro, horrified now by the way things were going. An old pro in trouble plays for time, you can't pin him easily. He knew every one of his rights, he stood on them all, he threw up dust. The Hon. David Lawney, he said, was out of his mind. Something to do with in-breeding. Johnson, too, was keeping mum. Another good pro.

Well—the Chief did the only things he could, really. He said: 'Get on to the city—tell them I'll be obliged if they will send a few patrol cars, to keep an eye open.'

'They can't get into the centre, sir,' Rolly Rawlins pointed out, 'unless we call the parade off.'

On what grounds, for God's sake? Burbling of a

drunken maniac who for some reason kidnapped his own wife and locked her in an attic? If no robbery took place or was attempted, that's what they'd say he over-reacted upon. 'I am well aware of that,' the Chief barked. Spoken like Napoleon. 'Have them block the roads out of town. And our own men—they have their personal radios. I want every one warned to look out for anything suspicious. Make sure we have a couple outside each of the banks, it could be a bank job. Runners—send runners out, to make sure nobody misses the radio message.' Good thinking, those puky little sets go often on the blink. And another good thought: 'Jewellers. See that we have somebody adjacent to all the jewellers.'

If British policemen clicked heels and said *Ja, mein Kommandant*, his two high henchmen perforce would have done it. Teutonic autocracy crackled in the Chief's voice. They spun away, bearing in their hearts deepened respect. Let there be no cock-up, here was a man with the chopper in his hand. They hadn't heard him bark like that before. He'd never been one yet, but given the right reasons one would say he could be a bastard.

Sergeant Rosher, when he had booked Mr Croker and the silent Johnson—no booking for Mrs Croker, but she'd face now a session of very difficult questions—had been sent on his way by a Percy well piqued by the kudos accrueing to his old enemy for (a) finding the van; and (b) sniffing out Croker and arresting him while he, Percy, peered through the cracks in a barn at Hutton Fellows. No complimentary speeches from those narrow lips. The superintendent, motored back post-haste, merely snapped: 'All right, Sergeant—that will be all. If we need you, you will be contacted.' And the sergeant went off into the busy streets, well content. Never mind the curt dismissal—by the book, the matter had to be taken from here by high brass, it was too big for lowly sergeants; but *he* found the van, and he had ready in his mind the written report telling how he went to Hutton Fellows in his own unpaid time, having formed a suspicion about that van . . . And *he* made the arrest. Could well be balance-tipper. Could well be that soon he would no longer be sergeant.

He went to the town square and mingled himself in with the crowds gathered and still gathering under the sun, shirtsleeved constables patrolling the single strand of rope erected as barrier between roadway and kerb. Everybody very affable, crowd and police and even Rosher himself. Not a bad old town, he thought. Looks pretty good, all the bunting. He even hoped, in a nebulous sort of way, that all these honest people would enjoy themselves. And this shows the self-gratified condition he was in.

He carried no personal radio. Plain clothes men prefer not to, sudden buzzing from an inside pocket is a dead giveaway. It was one of the uniform men who passed the message on, saying: 'Had the buzz, Sarge?'

'What buzz?'

The copper spoke low because of the nearby people. 'They reckon somebody might try to pull a stroke.'

'What kind of stroke?'

'Dunno, they didn't say. Eyes skinned for anything suspicious.'

'When you've done as long as I have, Sonny boy,' the sergeant said, 'you've *always* got your eyes skinned.' And he went his way, only man in all that town wearing a black hat and a durable blue serge suit, with the double seat and reinforced cuffs. Silly old twat, the constable thought.

The truck. Or van, if you prefer. It was actually a 22cwt, and either designation is acceptable, except perhaps to the extreme purist. It turned off the bypass to trundle along the lane, and one of the pseudo policemen said to his walkie-talkie: Paella. Just that, squawking through static, to make the man in uniform stationed where the sub-lane turned off re-position his diversion sign. He then stood waiting; and when escort and quarry came into view, he point-dutied them to follow the sign.

Two hundred yards along the sub-lane the two front motor-cyclists tumbled over a rope that jerked up suddenly before their wheels out of concealing leaves and earth. Neither was hurt, their speed was no more than twenty miles to the hour; but before they could move the men who jerked that rope materialized from bushes and stood over them, pistols ready, nylon stocking masks squashing their faces monstrously. The truck stopped short, having no room to pass without running over a recumbent body. Two more nylon-stockinged men carrying hardware materialized, one to train his sawn-down shotgun on the cab, the other covering with his the rearguard motor-cyclists, who came to a halt, raising their hands. From behind a bush Roddie Girdon-Ramsey watched the action.

Simplicity is the basis of all expert planning. Mr Croker, having the advantage of a good man on the inside who actually supervised the van's loading and passed along by radio the exact time of its setting forth, planned well. In no time at all, almost before the unofficial panda car drew up with its crew, nylon-stockinged like the rest and struggling into ordinary clothing, the four motor-cyclists were trussed and gagged and lying in the bushes, together with the truck driver and his mate. No snags. Now the raiding party split up, solid professionals who knew what to do without need for a single word spoken. Two alighted from the wolf car, ripped off its sheep's clothing and climbed in again. The now unremarkable black saloon reversed to where a passing recess gave room to turn and did so, headed for the bypass and London with a complement of casually clad men. A boot filled

with police clothing, but who would be looking in the
boot?

The other pistolleros, all the trussing done, moved
through the wood to a clearing where stood a blue Vaux-
hall Viva. They mounted and drove down a track to the
lane, and here they waited. By this time Eddie Langdon
was in the van driving seat. He called to the boy Girdon-
Ramsey, still lurking in his hedge: 'All right, kid—don't
hang about.'

The boy came forth, shaking with fright. This sort of
thing was not at all his scene, he much preferred drugs
work, little parcels distributed in car parks or lay-bys
from his quick-visiting motor-caravan. Not that he had
any aversion to violence. On the contrary. But he
favoured exercising it himself, and not in public lanes
close to home.

'Come on, come on,' Eddie snapped as the boy
scrambled to where the passenger sits. 'Cop hold of this.'
He shoved into the boy's hands his sawn-off scatter gun;
started the engine. 'All right,' he said. 'Start directing.
And keep your fingers off them fucking triggers. Parsons
Lane. Where is it?'

'You'll have to turn round,' the boy told him. 'It's the
other side of the bypass.'

Eddie reversed to the passing recess; turned, and they
drove away, followed by the car, in a truck very
unremarkable, chockablock with goodies.

Boxes of gold bullion lay in there, acquired by a rich
man with international contacts to afford unofficial tax
relief and a hedge against inflation. There were paintings
by Van Gogh, Corot, Constable, Velasquez, Picasso; and
a glorious triptych by Van Eyck, all bought not for love of
art, but for the same ignoble reason. And little leather
bags of splendid jewels, among them a diamond of no less
than 137 carats. Worth a king's ransom, that one alone.

And these were the articles clawed in by more or less

legitimate avarice. There were others, too. Do you remember a 12th-century illuminated bible, vanished from Winchester Cathedral? That was in there. And a beautiful mint-condition Saxon drinking bowl, gone missing from the Waverley Hoard? Aye—inside there, with various other things. All, in the right market, close up to priceless.

So how did all this lovely loot come to be riding around in a plain van guarded only by four outriders, two of whom fell over a string and all of whom were trussed in a trice?

The answer is simple. A man on the inside.

His name was Parvis, and he worked as private secretary to Sir Roland Goy, who made more money than Crœsus out of armaments. How a secretary so bent got into such a job does not matter—he did, it was his speciality, and set about winning trust; his idea at that time being to clear the house of what he could and scarper. Straightforward country mansion robbery. He'd done it before, often.

Well: Sir Roland, he found, was planning a move from this house to another fifteen miles away, on the coast. Armaments multi-millionaires grow old, which is more than can be said for many who sample their wares; and Sir Roland was old. Damn nearly senile. Had he not been, of course, not even the personable Parvis, with all his charm and very considerable secretarial talent, could have worked the oracle.

The minds of rich old men become obsessed: with their justly corrupted health and with fear of losing the fruit of a lifetime's grasping. They also become fanatically mean, especially in small things. Paul Getty, it is said, had a pay-up box beside the telephone. Sir Bernard Hauxwell spent his declining years prowling the packing department of his enormous factory, swooping on bits of discarded string and unravelling them for re-use.

So: the move was proposed for two reasons. A doctor as

smooth and basically bent as Parvis himself—big fees and quack advice, to an old buzzard inevitably one foot in the box—prescribed sea air. And the house on the coast was, quite literally, a castle. Bristle it with anti-burglar alarms, and surely the lifetime's loot should be safe there? Also, it would be under the eye; and commonly, among all the other people rich old men come increasingly to mistrust, are bankers and their managers, who will surely break into the vault.

Now Parvis, when he realized the potential—all that gear coming to this house so that Sir Roland could check it, gloating from his wheelchair, before it went on—knew it was too big to handle alone; so he contacted his old associate, Mr Croker, who normally acted as his clearing house; and now the fruit of assiduous planning rolled along Parsons Lane, en route for Dunn's Yard. Losing it would kill the old bastard; but then, his whole life's work was murder.

But: four men only, guarding it? How came this?

Just as simply. Parvis himself was no mean psychologist, and Mr Croker was even better. Easy, once the secretary has plumped up enough cushions and pillows to have attained the status almost of trusted son, to use that ingrained avarice and fear, that senile meanness in small matters.

Beware, said Parvis, the Securicor van and a phalanx of guards. Such cavalcades attract attack—look—look—look at this newspaper—and you will surely lose your all. Send a Securicor truck out by all means, with deliberate ostentation; but in it, for the confounding of villains when they open it, nothing but empty cases; while your treasure, at no extra cost, scuds home via the unexpected route in an unmarked truck guarded by four men from the firm of specialists known to me, whom I shall personally hand pick. No more, for low profile's sake and to keep costs down.

So, on this day chosen because St Barnolph had taken over in Mr Croker's town, a well-guarded Securicor van drove away from this grand old house; and not long after, off went the truck in which now sat Eddie Langdon and Roddie Girdon-Ramsey with a shotgun on his knee.

'Where now?' snapped Eddie, as they came to the bottom of Parsons Lane.

'Turn right,' the boy directed; and this was the error that cost them the vital minutes.

Chater would have gone the other way, up Filbert Road and through two or three back streets. But then Chater, briefed, would have known that the direct route to Dunn's Yard, by the right turn, was blocked off today at the top end. The boy had not been abroad for a week, he knew nothing of fête-day controls. So half way up this Dennison Street they found a row of the little rubber pyramids set up by the police, and a uniform standing by, waving them to a left-turn diversion.

'Christ!' said Eddie; and obeyed the policeman's peremptory signal with all the hair bristling on his neck. The van swung into the side street, followed at a discreet distance by its attendant car. 'Fuck it—fuck it,' said Eddie. 'You'd better know the fucking way from here.' Because there seemed to be no way back on to course. For all he knew, all the approaches to the yard might be sealed off.

They were not; but the boy's intimate knowledge of the town was confined to the better areas. These streets were semi-slum. Instead of the planned three minutes, ten had elapsed before they got to Dunn's Yard. By the time they arrived, Mr Bootey and the float were gone. Not only this: there was no Mr Croker to direct them to the desired doors.

Seven minutes ago, with the innocent Mr Bootey taken away for a pre-drive pint by hospitable Johnson, they should have driven straight into the yard. A few minutes of hard graft and they should have been gone, van, car and all, the loot stowed under that convenient mound topped by two thrones. After the parade, floats would depart in all directions. This one would go back to where it came from, still carrying virgins, Britannia, the Statue of Liberty *et al*, who would all take tea with the Hon. David Lawney. Tonight, the jewels and light articles would be delivered by Johnson to young Roddie in a place miles away, for flying out. Never mind the bullion and heavier stuff, arrangements were made for them involving a load of hay.

But instead of a waving Mr Croker, all they found was a high, very grimy brick wall—these buildings went up in 1868—inset with no fewer than five identical sets of enormous timber doors. 'Which is it? Which is it?' said Eddie. They just hate this sort of thing, criminals do.

'I don't—I don't—I don't know,' said Roddie. He was finding it difficult even to speak through all that bile-churning fear.

The van was at halt, the car stopping behind it. 'You stupid bastard,' cried Eddie. 'You twat—you'd better bleeding well find out—you're supposed to *know*.'

His glare, his rage, his murderous eyes set Roddie fumbling at the door handle. Wonder the shotgun didn't go off, handled like that. As he half fell into the road one of the men from the car approached, running. 'What's up? What's up?' he said.

'I—I—I—' said Roddie.

Eddie spoke from the cab. 'He don't know which fucking door it is.'

'Where's the fucking geezer?' said the man.

'How the hell do I know? Ain't here, is he? Try all the fucking doors.'

The man ran back to the car. Spoke. Out piled his three co-riders. They rushed to try doors. Roddie joined them.

Now the bent mind, very quick and agile sometimes within its pre-planned field of endeavour, does not always cope like lightning with sudden improvisation. All these men went to the same pair of doors; and finding them locked, charged on to the next. More time lost. It was Eddie, snarling from the cab, who had them scatter at last, one pelting along to the far end doors, one to the next, and so on. Roddie leaned against the first pair tried, being actively sick.

The men regrouped beside the van. 'All locked,' they said; and one said: 'Pick 'em—pick 'em.'

They were all skilled men, and not many professional villains have trouble with your simple padlock. In short time doors were opening, enough for a man to squint into the yard beyond. They all came rushing back. 'Nothing,' they said; and 'Empty,' and 'Sod all.'

Not without cause, a certain panic was beginning to spread itself around. This was no place to be lumbered with a load of loot. Fair enough on the right-hand side, nothing but the high wall, beyond it empty yards and these old buildings fronting on to Calum Street. But to the left it was open terrain, across scrapyards to the backs of houses. Eyes used to assessing risks looked, and disliked what they saw; particularly since the only way out was back along the cobbled alley by which they came in. Ahead, the cobbles terminated at a brick wall right-angled from the rest. Eyes swung to their leader.

'Out of town,' said Eddie. 'Into the country—hide away somewhere till I can find out what's going on.' They couldn't just sit here, he had to do something.

There was room along the alley to turn. The men ran for the car. It and the van reversed to a scrapyard entrance; turned and began to move back the way they came with the car now in the lead.

Roddie Girdon-Ramsey, done with spewing but over by the wall still, finding himself forgotten and about to be abandoned—which, thinking clearly, he could have considered no bad thing, he might simply have walked away—leaped in terror for the truck. Too late to gain the cab; but he screamed: 'Wait for me—wait for me,' and bashed on the metal side with the fist still holding the shotgun. The gun went off, and his soul flew out of his body so fast it never knew what killed him. He fell in the alley with half his head blown away.

Eddie heard the explosion, his wing mirror told him what had happened. 'Fucking hell,' he said, and drove on, turning left out of the alley in the wake of the car.

Oh, they badly needed Chater. Even Roddie, transferred to the forward car, would have turned them right. Chater probably would have told them not to move at all, to run that gear into one of the empty yards and sweat out rethinking time in there, out of sight; because although at first looking a left turn out of that alley must lead to open country, in fact the peculiarity of Calum Street is that it terminates at the far end of those buildings, as does the alley on the other side, in a blind brick wall. Access to open country is in the opposite direction—and you have to go through the middle of town, if you don't know the back streets.

Genuine panic must have come to those men when they realized there was a wall. The car made a hurried three-point turn and squealed away too fast up Calum Street as a nervous foot sought out from this potential trap, soon as possible. The van followed—too close, and also too fast. Eddie, shaken to the follicles, did not relish being alone. Automatically he sought closeness to the herd. Parked in a side street beyond where the police had blocked off the far end of the road before it reaches the town square, enjoying a covert smoke before resuming general patrol, Constables Wally Wargrave and Gordon Kenton saw them go by. 'Suspicious?' said Wally. 'Could be,' his oppo answered, and they dimped their cigarettes. Constable

Kenton set the wheels in motion.

How rightly Mr Croker opined that the job would benefit from a local guide. A dreadful strain on tight nerves, finding a police car coming up from behind when you are bent, and red-handed, and don't know where you are or even where this road goes to; until suddenly there is a line of little rubber pyramids from pavement to pavement, with a copper in the midst of them, holding up a hand.

Not entirely fair to say that the car driver (Frankie Fisher, his name was) panicked utterly. Nor did the other men. They simply did what crooks in such circumstances usually do, shot through with alarm. In cold sweat, yes; but not in blind terror. Down went Frankie's foot and the car leaped forward. Close behind, the van followed. Prudently, the policeman dived sideways.

Up got the copper and blew a whistle. Constable Wargrave turned his siren on. Faster than before, the car and van sped along Calum Street towards the bend which hides, from here, the town square.

They would roast Wally Wargrave later for that siren. It spurred the quarry on; and the square was packed with innocent bystanders.

Sergeant Rosher was standing on the corner, where Calum Street enters the square. The parade was on; first a mounted policeman riding a dapple horse generally called, because he cunningly stepped on grooming feet, You Bastard; then the Mayor and Mayoress in an open Rolls-Royce, relegating to third place St Barnolph, on his white horse as usual; and behind him all the floats. They came up the street called Fishgate, crossing the end of Calum Street to circumnavigate the square, leaving it by Bondgate, which runs parallel to Fishgate. So the leading floats were quitting the square as the later ones arrived in it.

The Hutton Fellows float came up Fishgate, as smartly

turned out as any. The Statue of Liberty stood before her throne, smiling and waving; showing rather more animation, perhaps, than would have been approved by Washington. There's young Hopper, the sergeant thought, walking alongside. Looks worried. He doesn't need to, she's all right. Bit wobbly, perhaps, but not so you'd notice. Far from pissed. And then he heard the siren and turned to see a car and a truck heading fast this way where no vehicle should be.

He gave not one thought to the eyes-skinned command. To be truthful, he did not think at all. It simply registered in his long-service-saturated brain that here were oafs, probably stoned, ignoring lawful prohibition. He jumped into the road, arms raised. The car swerved round him, accelerating; went straight on in a squeal of rubber.

Lucky, that car. Well handled, too. Frankie was a man picked for driving skill. The Hutton Fellows float by now was almost into the square, but the gap between it and the crowded pavement at the junction with Fishgate was hardly a car's width. Nevertheless, Frankie shot through it, to screams and a couple of faintings. And he did it again, weaving between the floats passing into Bondgate. Those men got clear away. Not that it did them much good, they were nicked within the hour not far from Wolverhampton.

The truck was not so lucky. Eddie, as a driver, was not in the Frankie Fisher league. Where Frankie kept his mind on that gap even as he swerved, finding the black-hatted ape-shape waving in his way Eddie allowed concentration to wobble. 'Oo fuck,' he sobbed, and trod hard down, driving straight. Rosher, in his mind, made echo. 'Oo fuck!' And he dived full length into the gutter.

Now Eddie was wrestling the wheel; because a straight line was all wrong, except to scatter the ape-man. Virgins were screaming now on the float, John Bull and Uncle

Sam were bracing, Britannia was hanging on tight; but when the truck hit—a glancing blow at the rear of the contraption, where there were, thank God, no people—as Eddie pitched forward, knocking himself cold on the windscreen, the Statue of Liberty was still standing, enjoying every hazy second of this happy day. She staggered as the float lurched; fell head first into the roadway. 'Oh, Jesus Christ!' said Patrolman Hopper, and rushed to where she lay.

Sergeant Rosher was also rushing, in rage, to do another thing that strengthened considerably the case for his re-elevation. And he didn't even know he was doing it. All he knew was: the bastard tried to run him down. So he pounded to the truck just as Eddie struggled upward out of black mist, and tore open the door, snarling 'Take that, you bastard,' as with his mighty hammer—oh, the fist on him, the terrible fist—he struck the poor man down again, thus subduing and apprehending, unarmed, a desperado with a pistol in his pocket.

Beside the float, among fallen virgins wailing from fear and bruising, Hopper crouched above the still body of his wife, saying over and over: 'Oh Christ—Oh Christ—Oh Christ—' A crisp man strode from among the stunned and seething crowd. 'Permit me,' he said. 'The name's Barton. I'm a doctor.' He knelt down, never mind his light grey hopsack trousers, there and then in the roadway.

CHAPTER 15

A few days later, with the weather broken back to British summertime normal, young Detective-Inspector Alec Cruse stood beside Patrolman Hopper in the airport departure zone, gazing through a panoramic window at hangars and aircraft standing about in the teeming rain and wishing he was a touch more senior and crafty, so that somebody else had been elected to the task of final farewell. What the hell could one talk about, things being as they were? All very well to mumble fittingly in company at the official gathering just concluded back at the station. Another thing entirely, alone with the poor bastard on a day of pissing rain.

'You—er—go from here via London, then, do you?' he said.

'Heathrow, yeah,' said Hopper. Not so liberal, these last days, with the flashing teeth. 'Just to—er—change 'planes.'

'Uh-huh. You won't have much time to see the sights, then.'

'No. Only the airport.'

'Uh-huh. Not much joy in that, they all look alike.' Cast around, now. Rake about in the mind for another subject, that one just died. Seeking suitable matter, Cruse looked towards the self-opening doors; and found, with great surprise, a very familiar figure in a black hat worn with a battleship grey raincoat, entering on bandy legs. 'Ah,' he said. 'Looks as if your oppo Sergeant Rosher's come to see you off.' Well, well, well—surprise, surprise.

The sergeant approached. No smile lightened those simian features. On the contrary, they wore a grimness. With more surprise, Cruse thought: I do believe he's embarrassed. Fancy him being here at all, in his own time. Out of character. But—funny—they seemed to hit it off right from when I put 'em together. ' 'Morning, Sergeant,' he said.

' 'Morning,' Rosher gruffed; and spoke to Hopper stiffly. 'Thought I'd just . . . hrrrmph.'

'Yeah,' said Hopper. 'Sure. How's—er—everything? Mr Croker and—everything?'

'Sends his regards. And apologies. Very cut up. Never meant it all to go like that. He'll be on porridge for a long time, Henry will. Well—there it is, he shouldn't have tried to play in the big boys' alley.'

'I rather liked him,' said the American.

'Mmm. Greedy. That's what it is—they all get greedy.' A pause, and still no smiling. 'More likeable than most, though. I'll give you that.'

The warm and soothing Kensington contralto designed to calm butterflies in the belly came glowing over the speakers. 'Passengers for Flight 108 to London (she pronounced it Lun-dun, two equal syllables) are requested to proceed now to Gate Se-ven. Gate Se-venn.'

'Ah,' said Cruse, fighting relief away from his face, 'that's it, then. Off we go.'

'Yeah,' Hopper said. 'That's right. Sure.'

They turned to where two hospital men were lifting a stretcher from where they had been guarding it, close by. Inspector Cruse, Sergeant Rosher removed their very different hats. The sergeant said nothing; but Cruse spoke.

'Goodbye, then, Mrs Hopper. I—we all—hope you will—er—make a full recovery. Very soon.'

She looked up, those great eyes made darker than ever by the white plaster cap fitted over her fractured skull, the thick metal collar holding in position a broken bone in her neck. Unexpected, the almost mocking smile she made. 'Goodbye. Thanks for a lovely party.'

Cruse turned now to Hopper. 'Well—good to have had you with us, Mr Hopper. Hope we'll see you again one of these days.' Gaylord. You couldn't say Gaylord, it had to be Mr Hopper, even now.

'Yeah. Thanks.' They shook hands; and then the young man turned to Rosher. His teeth retained the smile; but his eyes, his white face were not joining in. He extended his hand almost tentatively. 'S'long, Al. And—thanks. Thanks for everything. Been a real pleasure.'

'Uhhuh.' Rosher applied for a brief moment his gorilla grip. 'Look after yourself, son.'

'Sure.' Hopper turned away; said to his wife: 'Here we go, then, honey.' Ambulance men, stretcher, wife and patrolman all moved away, entering through Gate Seven. Somewhere, jet engines began to shriek through the warm-up.

Watching them go: 'Does it pass off?' said Inspector Cruse. 'That kind of paralysis?'

'Dunno,' Rosher grunted, still with a grim look about him. And he should have been whistling blithely, the station was saying he was dead cert now for promotion. 'The hospital reckons it might.'

'Rough. Very rough.'

'Wouldn't want to be in their shoes,' said the sergeant; and he whipped out the dreaded handkerchief. The blast he gave stood up there proudly, right alongside those shrieking jet engines. As he wiped up afterwards, he added: 'Poor little sod.'

But he didn't say which particular Hopper he meant.